"So, Let's Do It," Brandon Said.

Do it? Paige sucked in a quiet breath. She hadn't said that out loud, had she? No, of course she hadn't. Was he some sort of mind reader? "E-excuse me?"

"You said we had to fit me for a tux, didn't you? Let's go."

Oh, the *tux*. "Yes, right. Of course."

"What did you think I meant?"

Paige refused to answer on the grounds that it would mortify her.

Dear Reader,

My husband teases me relentlessly, because while I'm working on a book, for those eight weeks or so, the characters become living, breathing people to me. I talk about them as if they are real, because to me they are. They share dinner with us, come up during our favorite television shows.

I first meet these characters when I plot the book. The relationship is very superficial at that point. I know where they're from, what they do for a living, where they went to school—basic stuff. When I begin writing the story, gradually I learn more about them, but they don't always make it easy.

Take Brandon for instance. He was so busy trying to hide his true identity from Paige that I had a hard time getting a read on him. I knew he was Ronald Worth's son, and Emma's brother. I knew he was very bitter toward his father, but I didn't really know why. And every time I thought I had him figured out, he would do or say something to completely confuse me! In fact, he kept me and Paige guessing all the way to the end of the book. I hope you have as much fun figuring him out as we did.

Best,

Michelle

MICHELLE CELMER

EXPOSED: HER UNDERCOVER MILLIONAIRE

Special thanks and acknowledgment to Michelle Celmer
for her contribution to The Takeover miniseries.

ISBN-13: 978-0-373-73097-1

EXPOSED: HER UNDERCOVER MILLIONAIRE

Recycling programs
for this product may
not exist in your area.

www.Harlequin.com

Printed in U.S.A.

Books by Michelle Celmer

Desire

*Royal Seductions
†Black Gold Billionaires

MICHELLE CELMER

Bestselling author Michelle Celmer lives in southeastern Michigan with her husband, their three children, two dogs and two cats. When she's not writing or busy being a mom, you can find her in the garden or curled up with a romance novel. And if you twist her arm really hard you can usually persuade her into a day of power shopping.

Michelle loves to hear from readers. Visit her website, www.michellecelmer.com, or write her at P.O. Box 300, Clawson, MI 48017.

To my readers

* * *

Don't miss a single book in this series!

The Takeover
For better, for worse. For business, for pleasure.
These tycoons have vowed to have it all!

One

The man had the bluest eyes Paige Adams had ever seen.

Not to mention killer biceps, wide shoulders and the kind of all-American rugged good looks that left women swooning. Herself included. And though she didn't usually go for men with facial hair, the neatly trimmed mustache and goatee just seemed to work. In fact, she could swear the temperature of her office rose ten degrees the minute her assistant, Cheryl, ushered him inside.

"Paige, this Brandon Dilson," Cheryl said. "Ana Rodriguez sent him by."

Paige shut her laptop, smoothed the front of her Kay Unger blazer and darted a glance at her reflection in the chrome pencil holder on her desk to confirm that the chignon she wore her hair in was still neatly in place. And of course, it was. She prided herself on her appearance. As an image consultant, always looking her best was a requirement of the job.

She rose from her chair, pasted on a professional yet warm

smile and stuck her hand out. "A pleasure to meet you, Mr. Dilson."

He enfolded it in his much larger one, gripping firmly, *possessively,* and when his ocean-blue eyes locked on hers, and his sexy mouth tilted up into a dimpled smile—God, she loved dimples—she nearly forgot her own name.

His dishwater-blond hair was naturally wavy and a touch shaggy. Long enough to graze his shirt collar. The kind of hair a girl fantasized about running her fingers through. He wore faded jeans, a cobalt blue T-shirt and cowboy boots. And he looked damned good that way.

"The pleasure is all mine, ma'am." His smile said he meant it.

When Ana, the director of Hannah's Hope, the local literacy foundation, called to say she was sending over their star pupil for a consultation, a hunky cowboy was the last thing Paige had expected.

Behind him, Cheryl bit her lip and discreetly fanned her chubby face, and Paige knew exactly what she was thinking.

Who is this guy and where can I get one?

"Can I offer you a refreshment, Mr. Dilson?" Cheryl asked. "Coffee, tea, bottled water?"

He turned the smile her way. "No, thank you, ma'am."

Manners, too. That was nice.

Paige gestured to the chair opposite her desk. "Please, sit down."

He settled in, folding one long, muscular leg over the other, looking completely at ease. If his literacy issues or lack of education embarrassed or made him feel uncomfortable, he certainly didn't let it show. The man oozed confidence.

She smoothed her skirt and sat primly on the edge of her chair.

"I think that might be the cleanest desk I've ever seen," Mr. Dilson said, resting his elbows on the chair arms and threading his fingers together over his impressive chest.

"I like to keep things tidy," she said. Almost to the point of being compulsive about it. If she had a therapist he would probably tell her it was a direct result of her chaotic adolescence. But her past was what it was, and rehashing it to a mental health professional wouldn't change it.

"I see that," he said, and something about the way he studied her made her want to squirm in her seat.

"I understand you'll be honored with an outstanding achievement award at the Hannah's Hope gala later this month. Congratulations."

"Seeing as how every grade school student can do what I just learned, I don't see the big deal, but they insisted."

Gorgeous, polite *and* humble. Three traits that went well together. There was nothing she detested more than an arrogant man. And she had known her share.

"Did Ana explain to you what it is I do for the foundation?" she asked him.

"Not exactly."

"I'm an event planner and image consultant."

One brow rose slightly. "Image consultant?"

"I help people look and feel good about themselves."

"Well, no offense, but I'm pretty happy with myself just the way I am."

And he had every reason to be. But in her experience everyone had room for improvement.

"Have you ever been in the spotlight before, Mr. Dilson? Given a speech on stage?"

He shook his head. "No, ma'am."

"Then my job is to give you an idea of what you should expect when you accept your award. To prepare you for the formal atmosphere of the gala. Which, as an event planner, I am also organizing."

"So in other words, you're going to see that I don't make a fool out of myself. Or the foundation."

She didn't think that was going to be an issue. With looks

like his, he would have a tremendous stage presence. She could see why Ana chose to use him as the organization's poster child. "So you feel *comfortable*," she said.

"Well, I'm not big on crowds. I usually prefer to keep things one-on-one. If you know what I mean," he said with a wink.

If he was trying to fluster her, it was working.

She pulled a notepad and pen from the top drawer of her desk. "Why don't you tell me a little bit about yourself."

He shrugged. "Not much to tell. I was born in California and raised all over the country. I've spent the last fourteen years working as a ranch hand."

She had the distinct feeling there was a lot more to his life than that. Like how he managed to make it into adulthood without learning to read. But she wasn't quite sure how to word the question. Hannah's Hope was a dream client. It could thrust her company, Premier Image and Planning LLC, into the big time. The last thing she wanted to do was offend their star pupil.

She chose her next words carefully. "How is it you came to work with the foundation, Mr. Dilson?"

"It's Brandon," he said, flashing her that easy smile. "And I think what you really want to know is how a man can make it to thirty without learning to read."

He might have had literacy challenges, but he was a smart man. "How did you?"

"My mom died when I was young and my dad worked the rodeo so we moved around a lot when I was a kid. When he did manage to enroll me in school, I didn't stay in one place long enough to learn anything. I guess you could say I fell through the cracks."

It was sad to think how far he could have gone had he been given the proper education. "What motivated you to seek help?"

"My boss said he would make me a foreman of the ranch, but I had to improve my reading skills first, so here I am."

"Are you married?"

"Nope."

"Children?"

"Not to my knowledge."

She shot him a look, and that sizzling smile tipped up the corners of his mouth again. She wondered if he had any clue how gorgeous he was.

"Just kidding," he said.

Oh, yeah, he knew. "So that's a no?"

"No kids."

"Significant other?"

One brow rose up. "Why? You interested in the position?"

Oh, he had no idea. But she'd sworn a *long* time ago when, thanks to her mom's latest bum boyfriend, they were kicked out of their dumpy trailer and forced to live in an even dumpier women's shelter, she would only date educated, financially successful men. The kind who wouldn't steal next month's rent from her purse and use it to buy drugs or cheap whiskey, or gamble it away on a sure-thing horse.

Not that she had reason to believe Brandon was anything like her mom's loser boyfriends. She was sure he was a perfectly nice man. And he was incredibly easy on the eyes. Like... tangy eye candy. The kind that fizzed in her mouth and made it water. He just wasn't the kind of man she would ever date. His financial situation aside, he was too...*something*. Too sexy and charming. She wasn't looking to be swept off her feet. What she wanted was a responsible, dependable, *safe* man. A man as driven and dedicated to his career as she was to hers. An equal. One who could take care of her if the need arose. Not that anyone ever had to before. She'd always taken care of herself. But it never hurt to have a backup plan.

"I only wondered if you'll need an extra ticket for the gala," she said.

"No, ma'am, I don't need an extra ticket."

It didn't escape her attention that he'd managed to answer,

yet still avoid the subject of a significant other. Not that it was important she know. In fact, it was probably better that she didn't.

"I don't suppose you own a tuxedo," she said.

He laughed. "No, ma'am, I don't."

The ma'am thing was going to get old fast. She set her pen down. "You can call me Paige."

"Okay…Paige."

Something about the way he said her name made her face feel hot. In fact, she was beginning to sweat under her designer suit. She seriously needed to check the thermostat. Maybe the air-conditioning was on the fritz.

Or maybe her internal thermostat had gone haywire.

She resisted the urge to fan her face. "With the gala less than a month way, the first item on our agenda is to get you fitted for a rental tux."

"With all due respect, that's not exactly in my budget."

She waved away his concerns. "I'm sure the foundation can cover the expense."

His brow pulled low. "I'm not looking for a handout."

"We're a charitable foundation. Helping people is what we do. And the benefit is a black-tie function."

His expression darkened. "Is that legal?"

His sudden change of demeanor, from playfully flirtatious to darkly suspicious intrigued her. "I'm not sure what you mean."

"A literacy foundation renting tuxedos for people? Sounds…unethical."

She hadn't really thought of it that way. But she doubted it would be a problem. "I'll talk to Ana about it. I'm sure we can work something out."

He seemed to acknowledge that as an acceptable answer. And though his behavior was the slightest bit…odd, she assumed it was just male pride.

She hoped he would accept the foundation's help, as it would be a damned shame to miss the opportunity to see Brandon in a tux. He was going to look fantastic. Although she didn't doubt that he would look even better wearing nothing at all. And the things he could probably do with that body...

"So, let's do it," he said.

Do it? She sucked in a quiet breath. She hadn't said that out loud, had she? No, of course she hadn't. Was he some sort of mind reader? "E-excuse me?"

"You said we had to fit me for a tux, didn't you? Let's go."

Oh, the *tux*. "Yes, right. Of course."

"What did you think I meant?"

She refused to answer on the grounds that it would mortify her. "Nothing. I just...I didn't necessarily mean right this minute."

He leaned forward in his seat. "No time like the present, right?"

"Well, yes, but..." She frowned, opening her laptop to check her calendar for appointments. "I have to check my schedule. I had several calls I planned to make this afternoon."

He narrowed his eyes at her. "Let me guess, you're the kind of woman who plans her workday down to the last minute."

He said that like she was some freak of nature. Living such a spontaneous and...*uninhibited* lifestyle, he couldn't possibly understand the pressures of the corporate sector. But she wasn't totally incapable of compromise. She typically required several days' notice for this sort of appointment, but if she moved a few things around, and stayed an extra hour at the office, she could make it work.

It's not as if she had anything pressing waiting for her at home. Not even a pet. She was allergic to cats and considering the hours she worked, a dog was a responsibility she simply didn't have time for.

"I suppose I could squeeze you in," she told him. "But I'll need to have a word with Cheryl first."

"How 'bout I meet you outside?"

"Sure. I'll just be a minute."

They stood at the same time. Even in her three-inch Manolo Blahnik pumps, he was a good five or six inches taller. She wasn't normally intimidated by tall men. She wasn't intimidated by *anyone,* but something about him put her on edge. The fact that she had to walk past him to get to the door made her nervous.

What did she think he was going to do? Pull her in his arms and kiss her stockings off?

If only.

Being around a man so blatantly sexy was a stark reminder of how long it had been since she'd had any male attention. Of *any* kind. She'd been so busy the last few months, she hadn't had time to even think about dating. And sex? Hell, she could barely recall how long it had been since she'd had any. Any worth remembering, that is.

How sad was that?

She was willing to bet that Mr. Dilson could put a very pleasurable end to her dry spell. But he wasn't relationship material and she wasn't a one-night-stand kind of woman. Besides, she *never* mixed business with pleasure.

All things considered, it would be in her best interest to do her job, and stay as far the hell away from Brandon Dilson as possible.

Anyone who claimed that posing as an uneducated ranch hand to decimate the reputation of a bitter rival didn't have its perks, had obviously never met Paige Adams.

Brandon Worth—or Brandon Dilson as the people at Hannah's Hope had come to know him—leaned against the passenger's side door of his pickup, soaking up the Southern California sun, considering this new development. When he'd made the decision to infiltrate Hannah's Hope and expose the foundation as a fraud, seducing one of their contractors hadn't been part of the plan, but a man had to do what a man had to do.

Maybe by getting closer to Ms. Adams he would uncover the nefarious practices he suspected were driving the success of Hannah's Hope. And in the process he could finally bury its founder, Rafe Cameron.

If Brandon hadn't chosen to stay on the family ranch despite his father's failing health, Rafe may have never pulled off the very hostile takeover of Worth Industries, the manufacturing company that had been in his family for generations. Rumors were flying that Rafe planned to shut down the factory and sell it off in pieces, which would put more than half the city of Vista del Mar out of work and devastate the community. Brandon couldn't help feeling personally responsible. He let his bitterness toward his father overshadow his obligation to his hometown, to his legacy. Now he was determined to make amends.

Through Hannah's Hope, he planned to expose Rafe for the swindler that he was. Unfortunately, the volunteer he'd been working with the past couple of months knew virtually nothing about the inner workings of the charity. And he'd been careful to keep his distance from the Hannah's Hope office, for fear that his sister, Emma, who was on the board, might make a surprise appearance. He hadn't changed so much in fifteen years that his own sibling wouldn't recognize him.

Paige Adams could be his ace in the hole.

Paige emerged from the building, extracting a pair of designer sunglasses from a designer bag and sliding them on. She sure had a thing for labels.

He didn't usually go for the corporate type, but she couldn't be any worse than his gold-digging, soul-sucking, vampire of an ex-fiancée. And when they shook hands there were so many sparks flying he thought for sure the surface of her pristine desk would ignite.

He had the sneaking suspicion that beneath the designer suit and polished persona there was a wild woman lurking there, just itching to break free. And he would be more than happy to lend a hand. To run his fingers through her pale blond, upswept hair and mess it up a little. To kiss away that flawlessly applied lipstick.

He clearly made her nervous, a fact he would use to his advantage.

She spotted him leaning against the truck and strode over. She knew exactly where she was going, and how she planned to get there.

He grinned. They would just see about that.

As she approached, he opened the passenger door and gestured her inside. "Hop in."

She stopped abruptly, blinking behind her shades. "Oh, um, I thought we would meet there."

"No point in wasting gas if we're both going to the same place. Besides, parking is a pain this time of day."

She hesitated. Maybe she assumed because he couldn't read well, he was also a poor driver. Or maybe she just preferred to be in control. It made sense that anyone as well put together as Ms. Adams had to have at least a few control issues.

He flashed his most charming smile. "Don't you trust me?"

He could see her brain working to summon a response that wouldn't offend or alienate the foundation's star pupil. Then she peeked inside the truck. He wasn't sure what she thought she might find in there. Or maybe she worried she would dirty her designer clothes. The suit alone must have set her back at least a week's pay. Or maybe she was a trust-fund girl. The kind with a daddy who catered to her every whim, bought her everything her greedy little heart desired. He'd met his share of those at boarding school.

"I'll get you back in one piece," he said. "I promise."

Finally, she nodded and stepped past him to climb up. Quite a feat in her high heels, so he cupped her elbow to give her a boost, which gave him an awfully nice view of her nylon-clad thigh and—*hello*—was that a garter? Ms. Adams was an old-fashioned girl.

"Buckle up," he said before he shut the door and walked around to the driver's side. He got in and grabbed his own thrift-store sunglasses from the dash and put them on. Though he wasn't normally into labels, he did miss his Ray-Bans. "Where to?"

"The rental establishment is just a few blocks from here, off Vista Way," she said, looking even more on edge than she had in her office. "Do you know where that is?"

"Sure do." Though he hadn't lived in Vista del Mar since he was fifteen, when his dad sent him away to boarding school, he'd been in town long enough to relearn the area. Not much had changed. He backed out of the parking spot and maneuvered out of the lot into the heavy afternoon traffic. Paige sat awkwardly at the opposite end of the bench, spine stiff, nails digging into the edge of the seat.

He looked out the side window to hide a wry grin.

She was clearly the kind of woman who thrived on order and discipline. Being in control. And maybe it was a little depraved, but as he was pumping her for information, he just might have a little fun knocking her world off its axis.

Two

For a man who spent his time isolated from the world taking care of horses, Brandon sure did have a way with people.

The store she took him to for the fitting had recently opened, and Paige had been wanting to try it out, but twelve minutes after they walked through the door she knew she wouldn't be coming back. The salesperson, a dour-looking older woman with a perpetual frown, was on the phone when they walked in and didn't even acknowledge them. Five minutes later, when she did finally hang up, she went directly into the back room, still with no acknowledgment that they were even there, and didn't come back out for another seven minutes.

When she finally approached them she was snooty and condescending and looked down her nose at Brandon. If that wasn't bad enough, she actually rolled her eyes when Paige told her they were on a budget and wanted to see the bargain rack.

She was so rude that Paige had half a mind to walk out and take their business elsewhere. But after a few minutes of

Brandon's teasing and flirting, he had the woman giggling and blushing like a schoolgirl. It was truly fascinating to watch. And though Paige wouldn't have believed it possible, when he mentioned the tux was for a charitable event, she even offered to upgrade him to a more expensive brand for no extra cost. Then Brandon mentioned that Paige was an event planner and the woman must have seen potential future revenue. She became friendly to the point of being sticky sweet. Paige doubted she would ever return, though. Having a salesperson treat her clients rudely, even for five minutes, reflected badly on her company. It was a chance she couldn't take.

"So, that was an interesting experience," Brandon said when they were in the truck and on the way back to her office.

"I should apologize. I've never used that store before. And I never will again."

"Why not?"

"After the way she treated us when we came in? It was totally unprofessional. And I don't understand how you could be nice to her when she was so condescending."

He shrugged. "I like to give people the benefit of the doubt. Maybe she was really busy. Or maybe she was just having a bad day and needed someone to cheer her up."

"That's still no excuse to be rude to people."

He glanced over at her. "You can't tell me you've never had a bad day. Never snapped at someone who maybe didn't deserve it."

"Never a client."

"Well, you're a better person than most."

Or maybe she'd just learned to keep her emotions out of her business. And she considered it a shame that someone with Brandon's impressive people skills would be stuck in a career as a ranch hand. He could do so much more with his life if only he were properly motivated. Now that his reading skills had improved, he could get his GED and go to college.

Not that it was any of her business what he did with his life, she reminded herself. As an image consultant, helping people make serious life changes was a part of her business, and she loved what she did. But as Brandon had clearly stated earlier, he was happy just the way he was. And technically, he wasn't even her client. He only needed the skills to hold his own at the gala. Beyond that, she had no right sticking her nose into his life. It was just a shame to see all that potential go to waste.

She noticed that Brandon missed the turn back to her office.

"You should have turned there," she told him, gesturing in the direction of the street they'd just passed. Maybe, being unfamiliar with the area, he'd forgotten which route to take.

"I know where I'm going," he said.

"But that's the way back to my office. This route will take you several miles out of your way." And into one of the slightly less reputable parts of town. And she was on a tight schedule. It was already well after four, but she could probably sneak in a phone call or two before business hours were officially over, then do some internet research on a 60th anniversary party she was planning.

"Maybe I'm not taking you back to your office."

Her heart gave a sudden start. What was that supposed to mean?

What if getting in the truck with him hadn't been such a hot idea after all? What did she really know about him? He was attractive and charming, but so was Ted Bundy.

She glanced over at him. He leaned back casually, one hand resting on the steering wheel, the other propped in the open window. Not at all like he was about to pounce or pull a gun on her.

Just in case, she slid a little closer to the door, ready to shove it open the second the truck came to a stop if necessary. "Where are you taking me?"

He glanced over at her and grinned. "Relax. I'm not kidnapping you. I just thought I would take you out for a drink. Consider it my way of showing you my appreciation."

She let out a relieved breath and relaxed back in her seat. "That's really not necessary. Hannah's Hope will compensate me for my time."

"Well, I'd like to do it, anyway."

"I really need to get back to work."

"It's almost five on a Friday."

Four twenty-seven to be precise. And the longer they drove in the wrong direction, the later she would be getting back. "I planned to work late."

They stopped for a red light and he turned to her, looking puzzled. "Why?"

Because I have no life, was the first answer that popped into her head. Sad as that was. But that was not the reason. "I have obligations."

"Which I'm sure can wait until tomorrow." The light turned green and he accelerated. "Am I right?"

"Technically, yes, but—"

"So, wouldn't you rather be doing something fun?"

"Work *is* fun."

He raised a brow at her.

"You don't enjoy work?" she asked.

"Not on a Friday night," he said, giving her a sideways glance. "You look like a woman who knows how to navigate a dance floor."

Actually, she was a terrible dancer. She was so uncoordinated, she couldn't even manage simple aerobics. She was always two steps behind the rest of the group. "Well, I'm not. And I really need to get back to the office."

"No, you don't," he said. Just like that. As if she had no say in the matter.

He pulled into the lot of Billie's, a small, shabby-looking, country-and-western bar that she never would have ventured into on her own. Too many disturbing memories of pulling her mom, who was usually too intoxicated to walk unaided, out of a place just like it in the small Nevada town where she grew up.

And before she could insist that he turn the truck around and take her back to her office immediately, he was out the door and walking around to her side.

He pulled it open and held out a hand to help her down.

"I can't do this," she said.

"It's just one small step down to the ground," he said with a dimpled grin. "I promise I'll catch you if you fall."

The mischief in his eyes said he knew that wasn't what she meant, and his teasing grin warmed her from the inside out. Did the man have to be so adorable?

"I have a strict policy of not socializing with clients."

"That's a good policy. But I'm not one of your clients."

Damn it, he had her there. "But Hannah's Hope is my client, and by extension, so are you."

It was a flimsy excuse at best, and she could see that he wasn't buying it. She expected some snappy comeback, but instead he sobered, his eyes earnest.

"The thing is, I don't know a lot of people in town and it can get lonely sometimes."

Wow. She hadn't been expecting that. That kind of brutal honesty. He was making it really hard to tell him no.

"I'm sure there are any number of women in there who would be happy to have a drink with you." Among other things.

"But I want to have a drink with *you*."

She couldn't deny hearing those words, seeing the earnestness in his eyes, was just a little thrilling. And strangely enough, she wanted to get to know him better. There was something about Brandon that fascinated her. And not just his good looks, although she couldn't deny she was attracted to him.

How sad was the state of her personal life when a gorgeous, sexy man asked her out for a drink and she wanted to work instead? When had she become so obsessed with success that she couldn't take a few hours off to have a little fun?

Or, she could look at it from a profession angle. Brandon had so much potential. Maybe if they got to know one another, she could encourage him to do something more with his life.

It was only a drink, right?

"One drink," she said. "Then you'll take me right back to the office."

"I promise." Wearing a grin that said he'd known all along he would get his way, he held out a hand to help her down. His hand was big, and a little work-roughened. A sturdy, capable hand. And as it closed around her own, she had the strangest feeling of…security. As if she instinctively knew that, while she was with Brandon, he would never let anything hurt her.

How ridiculous was that? She barely knew the man. Besides, she was more than capable of taking care of herself.

As soon as she was on stable ground she let go. But as she picked her way across the gravel lot in her three-inch heels, it occurred to her how inappropriately she was dressed. The older-model cars in the lot said this wasn't the sort of establishment where business types hung out. In her suit, she was going to stick out like a sore thumb.

"You look nervous," he said as they approached the door.

"I think I'm overdressed."

"Trust me, no one will care."

He reached for the door handle and a rush of memories washed over her. A hazy, smoke-filled room teeming with the sour stench of stale liquor and hopelessness. Country-and-western music blaring at a decibel so loud one could barely think, much less hold a conversation—not that anyone went there to talk. She imagined couples grinding against each other on the dance floor and embracing in dark corners, doing God only knows what.

As Brandon pulled open the door she actually cringed, half expecting to see her mother there, slumped at the end of the bar, hands around a tumbler of cheap whiskey. But what she saw inside wasn't at all what she'd expected. Despite it's run-down exterior, it was clean and well-kept. The music was at a respectable level, and the air smelled not of smoke and liquor but smoked meat and spicy barbecue sauce.

Several men sat at the bar watching some sporting event on an enormous flat-screen television, but most of the booths were empty.

"Over there," he said, gesturing to the area beside the de-serted dance floor. She nearly jumped out of her skin when he put a hand on the small of her back to lead her. Did he have to be so touchy-feely? It wasn't professional.

And having a drink with him *was?*

She didn't want to give him the wrong impression, lead him to believe she was interested in anything but a professional relationship. She was sure she'd made that clear.

She slid into the seat of the booth he chose and he sat across from her. A waitress appeared to take their orders. She was an older woman with a pleasant face, wearing an apron that boasted Billie's ribs were the best in the west.

"Hey, Brandon," she said with a flirtatious smile. "You want the usual?"

"Yes, ma'am," he said.

She turned to Paige, giving her a quick once-over. The business suit clearly puzzled her. "And for your lady friend?"

Paige felt compelled to explain that she wasn't a "lady friend," just a business associate, although for the life of her she didn't know why it mattered what a virtual stranger thought. "A glass of Chardonnay, please."

"House okay?"

"Fine."

"Comin' right up," she said.

When she was gone, Paige said, "If she knows your usual, I guess you spend a lot of time here."

Brandon shrugged. "I'm in every couple of days. Like I said, it gets lonely."

"Where is it that you work, exactly?"

"Copper Run Ranch just outside of Wild Ridge."

"I've never heard of Wild Ridge."

"It's about two hours northeast of here, in the San Bernardino mountains. It used to be a mining town. Pretty as a picture."

"So you commute *four* hours every time you have a meeting with your mentor?"

"We meet twice a week, Thursdays and Sundays at the library. I drive in Thursday afternoon and stay in a hotel, then drive back to the ranch after my lesson on Sunday morning."

"And your boss is okay with you taking all those days off?"

"He's a generous man."

More generous than most. "How long have you worked for him?"

"Eight years."

"Have you ever thought of doing anything…different?"

"Like what?"

"I don't know. Going back to school, maybe."

"What for? I like what I do."

But didn't he want to better himself? He was obviously an intelligent man. He could be so much more than just a ranch hand.

The waitress returned with Paige's wine and a beer for Brandon. "Do you need menus?" she asked.

"No, thank you," Paige said.

"Are you sure?" Brandon asked. "Dinner is on me."

This was supposed to be one drink. Not a meal. "I really can't."

"Holler if you change your mind," the waitress said.

"Thanks, Billie," Brandon said as she walked away.

"Billie?" Paige asked. "As in the Billie on the sign outside?"

"That's right. She opened this place with her husband thirty years ago. They have two sons and three daughters. Their oldest son, Dave, is the cook and their youngest daughter, Christine, tends bar. Earl, her husband, passed away two years ago from a massive heart attack."

"How do you know all that?"

"I talk to her." He took a swallow of his beer and asked, "So, where are you from?"

"I grew up in Shoehill, Nevada." She sipped her wine, surprised to find that it was quite good. Usually "house wine" meant inferior.

"Never heard of it."

"It's a tiny, hole-in-the-wall town on the Arizona border. The kind of place where everyone has their nose in everyone else's business." And everyone knew her mother, the town lush.

"You still have family there?" Brandon asked.

"Distant relatives, but I haven't seen them in years. I'm an only child and my parents are both dead."

"I'm real sorry to hear that. Was it recent?"

"My dad died when I was seven, my mom when I was in college."

"How did they die?"

He sure did ask a lot of questions, and she wasn't used to revealing so much of her personal life to clients. Usually they were the ones doing all the revealing. But she didn't want to be rude. "My dad was in an accident. He was a trucker. He fell asleep behind the wheel and ran his truck off the road into an overpass. They said he survived the crash, but he was knocked out by the impact. He was hauling a tank of combustible liquid and it ignited."

"Jesus," Brandon muttered, shaking his head.

"My mom took it pretty hard." Her entire world had revolved around Paige's father. And instead of accepting his death and moving on, she'd crawled into a bottle instead.

"What did she do for a living?" he asked.

"Whatever paid the bills." Although thanks to her drinking, she never held a job for very long. They spent a lot of time on welfare.

"How did she die?"

"Liver cancer." Exacerbated by years of binge drinking. Not even a cancer diagnosis had been enough to sober her up. She'd given up without even trying to fight. In fact, Paige suspected that it had been a relief. That her mother had slowly been killing herself. That she would have ended it sooner if only she'd had the courage. And in a way, Paige wished she would have. She couldn't imagine ever being so weak that the loss of the man she loved could make her give up on life, and the welfare of her child.

She loved her mother, but Fiona Adams had been weak and fragile. All the things Paige swore she would never be.

"That must have been tough," Brandon said.

"I hadn't seen her in quite some time, and I was so busy with school I didn't really have time to be upset. I was a junior at UCLA and working to maintain a 4.0 GPA."

"Lofty goal."

"I had to keep my GPA up to keep my scholarship."

"Full ride?" he asked.

"Four years."

He sipped his beer. "You must be pretty smart."

He sounded impressed, like maybe he didn't meet a lot of smart people. "The hard work paid off. I graduated with honors and landed a job with one of the most prestigious event planning firms in San Diego."

"So how did you end up in Vista del Mar?"

"San Diego was pretty expensive for someone just starting out and my boss happened to own a rental place here. I liked the area so much that when I branched out on my own, I decided to base my business here, too."

"What made you decide to start your own business?"

She sipped her wine and said, "You ask a lot of questions."

He fished a nut from the bowl on the table and popped it in his mouth. "I'm curious by nature."

He was adorable enough to get away with it, and he listened with the kind of earnest, rapt attention that said he really cared. He seemed genuinely interested in knowing more about her.

"I was responsible for bringing in some of the firm's highest billing clients," she said. "Yet I was only seeing a fraction of the profit."

"So it was about money."

"Partially. I also wanted to branch out into image consulting, as well. And the truth is, I prefer to be in control." And it sure hadn't been easy. The high-end clients she was landing in her old job preferred the prestige and reputation of a larger firm. In the two years since she'd started Premier Image and Planning, Hannah's Hope was by far her largest, most prestigious account to date. The gala would draw in the organization's wealthiest contributors, including politicians and Hollywood celebrities. If she pulled it off without a hitch, and word got around, it could be the big break she'd been hoping for. So in essence, this single event could shape the entire future of her company.

"Sounds like you've done well for yourself," Brandon said.

"I've worked hard."

"How long have you worked with Hannah's Hope?"

"Since February."

"You're friends with Ana Rodriguez and Emma Worth?"

"No, I met Ana through a business contact. I coordinated a wedding for a friend of hers. She was impressed, and when she was looking for someone to plan the gala she remembered me. Emma I don't know well at all."

"How much do you know about Hannah's Hope?"

"Other than what they do for the community, and the information I need for the gala, not much. Why do you ask?"

"Just curious," he said, and gestured to Billie, who was taking an order a few booths down. Several more booths and tables had filled with customers since they sat down. "So, what do you do for fun?"

Hadn't they already covered this? "I don't really have time for fun."

"What do you do on your days off?"

"I don't take days off."

His brow rose. "Are you telling me you work seven days a week?"

"Typically, yes." She lifted her glass and realized she'd already sipped her way to the bottom. She hadn't meant to drink it so fast.

"Everyone needs a day off now and then," he said.

"It's not as if I don't ever take a day off. It's just that my business is at a crucial stage right now. The Hannah's Hope gala could make or break my career."

That seemed to surprise him. "It's *that* important?"

"Absolutely. With Ana's fiancé, Ward Miller, involved, and his name behind the organization, there will be music executives and Hollywood people attending. That's exactly the clientele I need to target in order to expand my company."

"I didn't realize it would be that big of a deal," he said, looking like the idea made him a little nervous.

"Don't worry. You'll do fine. I'll have you so well prepared, no one will ever guess you've never been in the public eye."

Billie appeared and set two more drinks in front of them.

"Thanks, Billie," Brandon said.

When had he ordered these? "You said one drink," she reminded him, glancing at the time on her phone. She'd already been away from the office longer than she should have.

"You're not enjoying my company?" he asked.

No, she was definitely enjoying it. For some reason, she felt comfortable talking to Brandon. Maybe because he really listened. She even liked the nervous, fidgety feeling she got when he studied her with those ocean-blue eyes. Even though it was wrong in more ways than she cared to consider. But a girl could fantasize, couldn't she? She could imagine how it would feel to be close to him. Even if it could never happen.

She had a plan. Her life was mapped out and there just wasn't a place for a man like Brandon. Although it sure would be fun to squeeze him in for a night or two. But everything inside of her was saying that would be a bad idea.

"I didn't say that," she said. "I just have a lot of work to do."

"What would happen if you didn't work tonight?"

"I'm not sure what you mean."

"Would your business crumble? Would the world come to an end?"

Now he was being ridiculous. "Of course not."

He reached across the table and covered her hand with his much larger one, fixing his gaze on her.

Oh, boy.

The look in his eyes, the warmth of his rough palm was doing funny things to her insides. To her head. How long had it been since a man's touch made her feel this way?

Way *too* long.

"Don't go back to work," he said, his eyes so warm and earnest she melted on the spot. "Spend the rest of the evening with me."

Three

Brandon knew he had her.

When he touched Paige's hand he could see her resolve draining away. Although he wasn't sure why he was so intent on getting her to hang around when it was clear that he wasn't going to get any information out of her in regard to the inner workings of Hannah's Hope. So why not cut her loose right now?

Because maybe what he'd told her about being lonely wasn't an exaggeration. He hadn't had a whole lot of female companionship lately. Hell, he hadn't so much as looked at a woman since he caught Ashleigh with his now ex-foreman going at it in the stable two days before their wedding last winter.

But he liked Paige. She wasn't what he'd expected when he first saw her, prim and proper behind her desk in her designer clothes. She was no trust-fund girl. It sounded as if she worked damned hard to be successful. And the fact that she would agree to go out for a drink with a man who was, as far as she knew, poor and uneducated, said a lot about her character. The fancy labels were for her clients, to give the appearance of professionalism, not because she was a snob. And he couldn't deny that was a refreshing change from women like his ex who spent thousands on their wardrobe for no other reason than to impress their friends. Or simply because they had money to burn. In his fiancée's case, *his* money.

Paige even reminded him of himself in a way. Isolated and obsessed with work. After the breakup he'd spent the majority of his time holed up at the ranch, seeing to the day-to-day operations. It was a rare occasion that he made it into town for any reason. Even a beer at the local brewery on a Friday night. He'd shut himself off from the world. And lately he'd been so obsessed with discrediting Rafe Cameron, he hadn't thought of much else. Only now, after meeting Paige, did he feel the desire for companionship.

But he had to be very careful where and with whom he let himself be seen. He couldn't risk being recognized and blowing his cover, not when he'd already invested more than four months in his plan. Especially if he planned to blow everything wide open at the gala—although at this point, there was nothing *to* blow open.

It seemed as if Paige was far enough removed from the people at Hannah's Hope, and from the rest of the world in general, that there was no threat of exposure when he was with her. And no one was bound to recognize him in this bar. No one he knew as Brandon Worth would be caught dead in a place like this. Personally, he preferred it over the Vista del Mar Beach and Tennis Club where his father and men like him drank eighty-year-old scotch and compared portfolios. Although after fifteen years he doubted anyone would recognize him. Just like he preferred being at the ranch, in the mountains, instead of cooped up in an office. He hadn't been built for the rat race. A trait he could only assume he'd inherited from his mother.

Paige sat across from him, gnawing the gloss from her full

bottom lip, but she didn't move her hand. Maybe she liked the way it felt wrapped in his. He did. In fact, if he had his way, they would be doing a lot more than just holding hands. Maybe it was finally time to end his self-imposed celibacy.

"I guess it wouldn't kill me to take one night off," she finally said. "But I do have to work in the morning so I can't be out too late."

"I'll have you home before my truck turns into a pumpkin, I promise."

"And just so we're clear," she said, easing her hand out from under his, "this is *not* a date. We can be friends, but nothing more."

"Friends it is," he said. The kind with benefits, maybe.

She relaxed back in her seat and took another sip of her wine. The bar was filling up. Soon people would be out on the dance floor, and at seven the band would start playing. And date or not, he had every intention of asking Paige to dance. A few more drinks and he was pretty sure he could persuade her into it. He could tell by her body language that the wine was already relaxing her.

She gazed up at him through the fringe of her lashes. Her eyes were quite extraordinary. Back in her office he could have sworn they were blue, but in this light they looked almost purple.

"You're staring at me," Paige said.

He leaned forward, resting his arms on the table. "I'm trying to figure out what color your eyes are."

"It depends on my mood. Sometimes they're blue, sometimes they're violet."

"What mood are you in when they're violet?"

"Happy. Relaxed."

He wondered what color they were when she was aroused, and if he would be lucky enough to find out.

"We've talked about me ever since we sat down. Why don't

you tell me about you," she said, then added, "And don't say there isn't much to tell. Everyone has a story."

He couldn't tell her his. Not the full version, anyway. But he knew the fewer lies he told, the fewer he had to remember, so it was best to stick as close to the truth as possible while still keeping up the charade.

"I'm originally from California," he said. "Not too far from here, in fact. My father lives pretty close by."

"Do you visit him?"

"Not in a long time. Suffice it to say we don't see eye to eye. About a lot of things."

"You said your mom died when you were young."

"Accidental overdose," he said. It had never been officially ruled a suicide, but only because she hadn't left a note. Anyone who knew Denise Worth knew she'd been miserable enough to take her own life. No thanks to his father and his extramarital affairs. Though Brandon had only been fourteen, her death had been the last straw, the final wedge in a relationship that had always been volatile in the best of circumstances. After her death, he and his father barely spoke. His mother had always favored Brandon, and his sister, Emma, had been daddy's little princess. And still was, as far as he knew.

"Do you have siblings?" Paige asked.

"A sister. But I haven't seen her in fifteen years." Not since the day he'd headed off to boarding school on the east coast. Although from what he'd heard, she'd married recently and was pregnant with her first child. He would be an uncle, but in title only. He doubted he would ever see the child.

"Fifteen years is a long time not to talk to a sister."

"It's complicated."

"It must be, because it's hard to imagine that someone as personable, as *nice,* as you, could hold a grudge for so long."

He grinned. "You barely know me. Maybe I'm only pretending to be nice."

She considered that for a second, then shook her head. "No.

You're forgetting, I'm an image consultant. I'm pretty adept at reading people. The way you handled saleslady sunshine earlier, that's impossible to fake. You're good with people. A *nice* guy."

Maybe *too* nice. Definitely too trusting. Ashleigh had taught him that, and it had been a bitter pill to swallow. But she was the last person he wanted to think about right now.

"So I guess you kinda like me," he said, grinning. "Since I'm such a nice guy."

"Maybe I don't like nice guys," she said draining her second glass. "Maybe I prefer men who are bad for me."

The wine must have been going to her head. She was starting to get flirtatious.

He leaned forward, locking his eyes on hers. "I'll have you know, I can be *very* bad."

Maybe it was his imagination, but he could swear the color of her eyes deepened. And he had the feeling this was about to get interesting.

"Why is it that a beautiful woman like you doesn't have a boyfriend?"

"Who says I don't?"

"If you did, you wouldn't have been planning to work on a Friday night. And you sure as hell wouldn't be here with me."

"I'm focusing on my career. I don't have time for a relationship."

Exactly the type of woman he needed right now. One who wouldn't want or expect a commitment. Paige was becoming more appealing by the minute. Most women came after him all pistons firing, talons out.

This was a refreshing change of pace. A woman who *didn't* have time for him. Of course, if she knew about the millions in his trust fund, she might make time.

"Why don't you have a girlfriend?" she asked.

He grinned. "Who says I don't?"

"If you did, you wouldn't be here with me."

Touché. "Until late last year I had a fiancée."

The teasing expression slipped from her face. "It didn't work out?"

"If 'didn't work out' is a polite way of saying that she cheated on me with the ranch foreman."

She winced and shook her head. "I don't understand people who cheat on their significant others. If you aren't happy with someone, why not just leave?"

Ashleigh had a couple million reasons to stick around. And according to her, she'd *never* been "happy" with him, or had any intention of being faithful. All she cared about was the money. Or so she had spat at him when he kicked her to the curb. But she'd sure had him snowed. She'd managed to convince him that he was the love of her life.

"Are you speaking from personal experience?" he asked.

"No, but my mom had boyfriends who couldn't seem to keep it in their pants. Of course, being with someone like my mom couldn't have been a picnic."

"Why is that?"

She hesitated, then said, "My mom was an alcoholic. She started drinking the day my dad died, and didn't stop until she drank herself to death."

"That must have been rough."

"She was weak and pathetic."

And obviously Paige resented the hell out of her for it, and he was guessing she would do anything to not be like her. To be successful and self-sufficient. Not the type of woman who used a man for his money. Not that he was in the market for a relationship.

Maybe it was time he lightened the mood a little. He gestured to Billie for another round, and since there happened to be a slow song playing, he slid out of the booth and held out his hand. "Dance with me."

Her eyes went wide and she shook her head. "No. I don't dance."

"Everybody dances."

"I'm serious, Brandon. I can't dance. At all."

"It's not difficult."

"For me it is. I'm the most uncoordinated person on the planet."

"When was the last time you tried?"

"Senior prom. I stepped on Devon Cornwall's feet so many times I ruined his rental shoes and he had to pay extra."

He raised a brow. "No, he didn't."

"Seriously, he did. I'm that awful."

"Well, you can step on my boots all you want. It won't bother me." He grabbed her hand and coaxed her out of the booth. But when he tried to pull her onto the floor, she resisted. "But no one else is dancing."

"We'll be trendsetters. In a couple of hours it'll be packed."

She darted a glance around as he led her out on to the deserted dance floor. "Everyone is watching. I'm going to make a complete fool of myself."

"Relax," he said, pulling her into his arms. She stood there stiffly, like she wasn't sure what to do. He took her hands, placing one on his right hip and the other on his left shoulder, then he put both hands on her waist and tugged her closer. She sucked in a quiet breath as their bodies collided, and damn, she felt nice.

He started slow, just swaying gently to the music. In her heels her eyes were level with his chin, but she was petite. She had a narrow waist and delicate, finely boned hands. But there was a sturdiness about her, and enough weight behind her to make him wince when she stepped down on the toes of his left foot.

"Sorry!" she said, her cheeks flushing. "I warned you."

The problem was, she was trying to lead. "Just relax and follow my steps."

For the first three quarters of the song he looked at the top of her head while she watched their feet, and she was doing pretty well, but the second she looked up she stepped on him again.

"Sorry!"

"It's okay. You're getting the hang of it. I'll have you line dancing in no time."

"Line dancing?" Her eyes went wide and she stumbled over his boot. He hissed out a breath as her heel ground into his big toe. "Sorry!"

"Watch my feet," he said and she lowered her eyes again. "And yes, line dancing."

"I definitely can't line dance."

"Anyone can line dance. It just takes practice."

"I'm seriously not that coordinated."

"You don't have to be. It's just simple repetitive movements."

She glanced up again and caught him in the opposite foot with her other heel. At this rate, she really would destroy his boots.

"Sorry!"

"I have an idea," he said. "Give me your foot."

She frowned. "What are you going to do with it?"

"I'll give it back."

She bent her leg up. He reached down and grabbed her shoe, slipped it off, and tossed it under their table.

"But—"

"Other side," he said, waiting patiently for her to lift her foot, and maybe she sensed that he wouldn't take no for an answer because she complied. He slid it off and tossed it with its mate.

"Why did you do that?" she asked.

He pulled her back into his arms. "They were getting in the way."

"I feel like so short without them."

She was significantly smaller with them off. The top of her head barely reached his chin. "How tall are you, anyway?"

"Five-three if I stand really straight. I've always wanted to be taller."

"Why? What's wrong with being short?"

She rolled her eyes. "Only a tall person would ask that."

"I'm only six-one."

"*Only.* You're *ten* inches taller than me!"

He grinned. "But have you noticed that since you took them off you've been dancing and you haven't stumbled once?"

She blinked. "I haven't?"

"I told you, you could do it."

She looked so thrilled, it made him smile, and she must have been happy, too, because her eyes were bright violet. But then a faster song started, and he wasn't sure she was up to the challenge just yet. One step at a time.

He led her back to the booth. Billie had left them fresh drinks and a set of menus.

"Think Billie is trying to tell us something?" he asked.

"I guess I am a little hungry," she said, taking a swallow of her wine, then another. She was going to have to pace herself or he would be carrying her out to the truck.

She ordered a salad and he got his usual burger. As they waited for their food the dance floor began to fill up. He thought she might be nervous dancing around so many people, but when another slow song began she actually got up and dragged him out of the booth and onto the dance floor, in her stocking feet this time. When he pulled her close, she didn't put up the least bit of resistance. This time she leaned in closer, and it didn't escape him how perfectly her body seemed to fit tucked against his.

"I think I actually kind of like this," she said, smiling up at him. She *was* getting better. She only stepped on his foot once through the entire song.

When their food arrived, they returned to their seats and

before she sat she shrugged out of her suit jacket, folding it neatly and laying it on the seat beside her. Underneath she wore a pale pink, silk shell tank that was as soft and delicate-looking as her skin. Her bust was on the small side, but perfectly proportionate to her size. Unlike Ashleigh, whose surgically enhanced chest had always been a source of mixed feelings for him. He preferred things natural. And while Ashleigh's implants *looked* good, there was nothing "natural" about them. They felt exactly like what they were, sacks of fluid stuffed in her chest. But it was one of those things, a minor glitch in the relationship that he'd been willing to overlook.

He couldn't help wondering how Paige's would feel. What was it they used to joke about in high school? More than a mouthful was a waste? Well, it looked to him as if Paige was just right.

She ordered a fourth glass of wine with her dinner and he could tell it was going to her head. But when he tried to get her to line dance she said she was too afraid of embarrassing herself. He pointed out that she would never learn if she didn't at least try, but that argument got him nowhere. Besides, she seemed to like slow dancing, and he liked holding her close. After glass five, she chucked the last of her inhibitions and glued her body to his, rubbing against him in a way that was honest-to-goodness torture, and she was giving off enough heat to melt the polar caps.

Since breaking his engagement, Brandon had barely looked at another woman, and he sure as hell hadn't been ready to sleep with one. Until now. He wanted Paige. But as far as she was concerned, he was an uneducated rancher with practically nothing to his name. The question was, did she want him enough to see past that?

This would be a test, to see the kind of woman Paige Adams really was.

Though Paige knew it was wrong, and there were a couple dozen really good reasons not to get involved with a man like

Brandon, she wanted him. Maybe it was the wine, or the fact that she hadn't been with a man in a very long time, but she couldn't seem to get close enough. She typically went for the studious type, who tended not to be so blessed physically, but Brandon's body felt so solid and strong. And he smelled so good. She even liked the feel of his beard against her forehead when she laid her head on his chest. She'd expected it to be wiry and sharp, but in reality it was soft.

"I guess you've got the hang of it now," he said. His voice had a husky quality that hadn't been there before, and when she smiled up at him, the look in his eyes said he wanted her, too.

"I'm glad you forced me to try."

"Me, too." He reached up and tucked a stray hair back from her face. It had begun to work itself loose from the chignon, which under normal circumstances would have had her running to the ladies room to fix it. Tonight she didn't care.

"Do you always wear your hair up?" he asked.

"For work I do."

"I'll bet it looks sexy down." He ran the fingers of both hands through her hair, pulling the pins loose so it spilled around her shoulders.

"I was right," he said with a sizzling smile that sent her internal temperature skyrocketing. "You probably hear this all the time, but you're a beautiful woman."

No, she hadn't heard it in a *long* time. If he kept saying things like that, kept looking at her that way, she was going to forget all the reasons this was wrong. Why they could only be friends. Which she suspected was exactly what he was hoping.

Their eyes locked, and though she knew she should look away, her gaze felt glued to his.

Was he going to kiss her? God knows she wanted him to.

He dipped his head slightly, and she lifted her chin to meet him halfway, but he only pressed his forehead to hers. Her disappointment, the desire to feel his lips on hers, to taste him, was almost too much to take.

The song ended and he took her hand, leading her back to the table. "It's getting late. I should get you home."

She looked up at the clock over the bar and was surprised to see it was almost midnight. Hours later than she typically stayed out. But she was having so much fun she hated to leave. Then again, if he took her home, maybe he would kiss her good-night. She knew she shouldn't let him, that it would be leading him on. There was no future for them. But the idea of his lips on hers was making her weak in the knees.

She put on her shoes and jacket and they walked out to the parking lot. She felt so unsteady on the gravel, he had to slip an arm around her.

"My car is still at work," she said.

"Yeah, but you're in no condition to drive."

"But how will I get to the office tomorrow?"

"I'll come by in the morning and drive you over there so you can pick it up."

Sounded like the perfect solution, because then she would have to see him again. Maybe that was the whole point. Maybe he wanted to see her again, too.

He helped her into the truck, then walked around and got inside. "Where to?"

She gave him the directions to her apartment complex. It struck her as very odd, as he drove her home, how comfortable she had come to feel with him. Considering they had known each other a grand total of nine hours. It usually took her time to warm to people, to let down her guard. To trust. She was a private person by nature, but she'd told Brandon things tonight that she'd only told her closest friends. People she had known for years. Even her secretary, who had been with her since she started her company, knew very little about Paige's childhood. Maybe because she and Brandon had similar dysfunctional pasts she felt comfortable confiding in him.

"You're awfully quiet," Brandon said, glancing over at her. "Everything okay?"

"Fine. I feel good. In fact, I haven't felt this good in a really long time. I had so much fun tonight."

"So did I."

When they got to her complex, he parked out front and walked around to open her door. As she got down, she wobbled on her heels and nearly lost her balance.

"Whoa!" He caught her under the arm, saving her from taking a header onto the concrete walk. "You all right?"

"I guess I'm a little tipsier than I thought," she said, clinging to his arm, feeling his hard muscle underneath warm skin. She couldn't stop herself from wondering how the rest of him felt. And what he would do if she tried to find out. After all the bumping and grinding they had done on the dance floor, at the very least she'd earned a kiss good-night.

They reached her door and he took her keys to unlock it, then he turned to her. "I had a real nice time tonight."

"Me, too." *Now kiss me and put me out of my misery.*

"Thanks for keeping me company."

"You're welcome." *Come on already. Just do it,* she urged silently, and something in his eyes said he read her loud and clear. He stepped closer, and the world seemed to slip into slow motion.

His head dipped down and her chin lifted. Her eyes slipped closed, and she held her breath, waiting to feel his lips on hers. Would it be slow and sweet, or reckless and wild? Would his lips be as soft as they looked? And how would he taste?

She felt his breath across her mouth, caught the clean scent of his aftershave, then felt the brush of his lips...*on her cheek?*

Huh?

He lingered there for a few seconds, his breath warm, his lips soft. Then he started to back away, but having spent the last several hours in a perpetual state of sexual excitement, a simple kiss on the cheek was *not* going to cut it at this point.

Shoving aside her last shred of good sense, Paige slid her arms around his neck, pulled his head down and pressed her lips to his.

Four

Paige sighed softly as Brandon's lips brushed against hers, slow and sweet. Tender. His beard and mustache tickled her. She'd never kissed a man with facial hair, but she liked it. In fact, it was the best first kiss she'd ever had. By leaps and bounds. And it had barely started.

He cupped her face in one of his rough palms, tunneled it through her hair, tilting her head for just the right angle, and deepened the kiss. She moaned as his tongue rubbed against hers, and all she could think was *more*. It was so perfect, she didn't ever want it to end.

His arms went around her, his big, capable hands easing her in closer against the hard planes of his body, and when she realized that he was aroused, she went hot all over. It took exactly two seconds to determine that a kiss wasn't going to be enough. She wanted to touch him, to feel him all over. She wanted him in her bed. She wanted to feel the weight of his body pressing her into the mattress as he drove hard inside of her.

She wanted it so much she *ached* for it.

She tugged his T-shirt from the waist of his pants, sliding her hands up underneath, flattening them against his hard, lean stomach, and he groaned against her mouth. She hadn't even seen his body, but already she knew it would be perfect. She started walking backward, tugging him inside with her, but he stopped abruptly at the threshold. He broke the kiss, taking her by the wrists.

"Paige, I can't."

What? Didn't he want her? He sure kissed like he did.

"Don't think it's because I don't want to," he said. "I do, more than you could possibly imagine, but you've had a lot to drink. I feel like I would be taking advantage of you."

Take advantage of me, please, she wanted to say. But he was right. She'd had a lot to drink. Way more than she ever did. Odds were good it was severely impairing her judgment.

Odds were good? *Of course* her judgment was impaired. She was inviting a client into her apartment with every intention of sleeping with him. A man who met not a single one of her dating requirements. Not that she'd had any intention of actually dating him. She just wanted sex.

Ugh! What was she *doing?*

"You're right," she said, backing up a step, out of his grasp, clutching the door frame for balance. "I don't know what I was thinking."

"If it's any consolation, I was thinking the same thing."

Somehow that only made her feel worse.

"Thank you for talking me into coming out with you tonight," she said. "I had fun."

"So did I."

"I hope we can still be friends. Maybe we could do it again sometime." Just without the kissing. And grinding. And the excessive amounts of alcohol.

"I'd like that."

And if she stood out here much longer, if she didn't get

inside, she was bound to launch herself into his arms. And if that happened, she wouldn't be accepting no for an answer.

Maybe he was thinking the same thing, because he said, "I should go."

"Thanks for dinner, and the drinks and teaching me how to dance."

"You're welcome. Thanks for keeping me company."

He looked like he wanted to kiss her again. He even took a step toward her, but something in her eyes must have warned him exactly what would happen if he did, because he turned, headed down the walk, his footfalls heavy against the concrete. He disappeared around the corner, and she listened until his footsteps faded—just in case he changed his mind and came back. When he didn't, when she heard the engine of his truck start, she stepped inside and shut the door behind her.

She'd almost made a huge mistake. Crossed a line she swore she would never cross. She'd dodged a bullet when Brandon put on the brakes, so why instead did it feel as though it had pierced her heart?

Holy hell.

Brandon sat in his truck, engine running, gripping the steering wheel, trying to calm his racing heart. What the hell had just happened back there? He knew Paige had spunk, and he knew that he was getting her hot and bothered on the dance floor, but he'd never expected her to throw herself at him that way. And when she'd kissed him… Jesus. He'd never connected with a woman like that before. Physically, emotionally—it was like a freaking religious experience. And putting on the brakes, telling her no, had been torture. In the sixty seconds it had taken him to walk back to his truck, he'd almost turned back at least a dozen times.

If she'd been even the slightest bit sober, he would have accepted her invitation without question. He would have her in bed right now. But it was good that he didn't. He was glad she'd had too much to drink, and he'd had an excuse to stop her.

What the hell had he been thinking? Had he honestly believed an affair with Paige was a good idea? He didn't have time for this. Time for her, or any relationship. Especially one that wouldn't bring him any closer to exposing Rafe Cameron. He was on a mission, and he couldn't afford any distractions.

But oh, what a stimulating distraction she would be. And he'd been right about one thing. Under the designer suit and polished persona there was a wild woman struggling to break free. And if he knew what was good for them both, he would stay as far away from Paige Adams as humanly possible.

He would drive her to work in the morning to get her car, then, besides in a professional capacity, it was the last he would see of his new "friend."

Paige woke the next morning with a brain-splitting hangover, but the relentless thumping in her skull as she sat up in bed was no match for the humiliation of her mortifying lapse of moral judgment.

What had she been thinking, drinking so much? Hell, she never should have agreed to one drink much less…was it five? Six? She'd lost count.

And even worse than the humiliation was the fact that she'd had so much…*fun.* The talking and the dancing. The *flirting.* She couldn't recall the last time she'd been so relaxed, and focused on something other than work. She couldn't forget the way Brandon's arms felt around her on the dance floor. The softness of his lips and the taste of his mouth when she kissed him. The hard length of his erection through his jeans as he pulled her close. She hadn't been too drunk to remember *that.* Or the way she had tried to drag him into her apartment.

If he hadn't been such a gentleman, hadn't stopped things before they went too far, she most definitely would have slept with him. He could be lying beside her right now, sleepy and rumpled.…

She shook away the mental image, regretting the move instantly as pain stabbed her temples.

She crawled out of bed and stumbled to the kitchen, swallowing three pain tablets with a huge glass of cold water. In the bathroom, she cringed when she saw her reflection. It was a good thing Brandon hadn't stayed over. With her puffy eyes, smudged mascara and hair askew, she would have scared him away for sure.

She showered, brushed her teeth and dressed for work, choosing her favorite skinny jeans and a soft cotton shirt. During the week she took great care in her appearance, but weekends, if she had no meetings, or events to attend, she kept it casual. She dried her hair and pulled it back in a ponytail, then swiped on mascara and a touch of lip gloss. She was considering whether she should make a pot of coffee or pick a cup up on her way to work when there was a knock on her front door. She couldn't imagine who it might be, since she rarely had visitors at nine-thirty on a Saturday morning.

Oh, hell, who was she kidding? She didn't get visitors *ever*. She didn't have time for friends lately. Her secretary was the closest thing she had to a confidant.

She opened the door, only a little surprised to find Brandon on the other side.

"Good morning," he said with one of those adorable, dimpled grins. The man was honestly too cute for his own good. He was dressed pretty much the same as the night before. Jeans, a T-shirt and cowboy boots, only this time he'd added a black Stetson to the ensemble. And he looked so delicious she wanted to eat him up.

Bad idea, Paige. Really bad idea.

In his hands he carried two jumbo-size cups of coffee from her favorite coffeehouse, and when the rich scent drifted her way, her mouth started to water.

She didn't bother to ask what he was doing there, as she had a pretty good idea already. After last night, he probably assumed they were starting some sort of relationship. Why wouldn't he? And she couldn't deny that the coffee was a nice touch. But she would have to set him straight, make it clear that last night was a mistake, and it wouldn't happen again. The chemistry aside, they were all wrong for each other.

And if it was so wrong, why was her heart suddenly going berserk in her chest? And why couldn't she seem to stop looking at his mouth?

"I thought you could probably use it," he said, handing her a cup. "Aren't you going to invite me in?"

As a rule, she didn't invite people into her home. Especially not business associates. All of her resources went into keeping up the proper appearance in public. There wasn't much left over for personal splurges.

But of all the people she could bring here, he probably cared the least about appearances. Besides, he was grinning that sexy smile and the coffee smelled so delicious. She just couldn't tell him no. At least this would give them a chance to talk about last night, to establish boundaries.

She moved aside, wondering what he was thinking as he stepped inside and gazed around at the small space. The secondhand furniture and threadbare carpet. It wasn't a great apartment, but the rent was reasonable and the area was safe, and the furniture may have been old, but it was *hers*.

"Nice place," he said. "Cozy."

She shut the door. "You mean small."

He turned to her. "No, I mean cozy. And I like it. I like that it's at complete odds with your professional persona."

Though she felt compelled to give him an explanation, she had the feeling he didn't expect or need one. Instead she gestured him into the tiny kitchen. "Do you need cream or sugar?"

"No, thanks."

She set the coffee down on the tiny square of counter space beside the two-burner economy stove and opened the cupboard to take out the sugar. "So, what brings you here this morning?"

"I told you I would pick you up this morning."

She looked at him over her shoulder. "Pick me up?"

"To get your car. You left it at work yesterday. Remember?"

"Oh, right." She had completely forgotten about that. Which wasn't at all like her. Wouldn't she have been surprised when she went out to the carport to find it missing.

Did that mean he wasn't here because of last night? That he was just being polite? That he wasn't interested in a relationship any more than she was?

If that was the case, it should be a relief, so why, as she dumped a heaping teaspoon of sugar into her cup, was disappointment burning in her belly?

There is something seriously wrong with you, honey.

"There was something else, too," he said. "Something I wanted to give you."

She set the spoon down and turned to find him right behind her, and the instant she saw the look in his eyes, saw him leaning in, she knew exactly what he was going to "give" her. Before she could utter a word, or make a move to stop him, his lips were on hers. So soft and warm and sweet.

At first, anyway.

It didn't take long for the kiss to deepen, and pick up momentum. His arms went around her, drawing her against him, and his tongue rubbed against hers, lulling her into a state of total sexual bliss.

Oh, my God.

She had been hoping that in her intoxicated state she had exaggerated how fantastic the kiss last night had been, only now she realized the opposite was true.

It was even *better* than she remembered.

In the span of a breath she was right back in that place where she wanted to put her hands on him, touch him all over.

So much for establishing boundaries. This was so wrong, so inappropriate. But how did one fight a tidal wave? A tsunami of conflicting emotions?

They parted slowly, lips lingering, as if neither wanted to be the first to end it. Brandon sighed and pressed his forehead to hers. "I promised myself I wasn't going to do that. But then I saw you...I just couldn't resist."

She wished he would have. He was making it really hard for her to do the right thing. "I was just about to tell you that last night was a mistake, and we can't see each other again socially."

"Yet, here we are."

That didn't mean it was smart. "This isn't going to work, Brandon."

"I know."

"We want completely different things from life."

"I know."

"And I just don't have the time for a relationship now."

"So let's not have a relationship."

"What, then?"

He shrugged. "Why don't we just...keep it casual, see where this goes. Have fun."

She didn't have time for fun. Although, last night *had* been really nice. Maybe occasionally it wouldn't hurt to relax a little and focus on something other than her career.

"I have an idea," he said, stroking her cheek with the backs of his fingers. "Why don't you skip work today."

"I can't." But she wanted to. She didn't want to think about caterers and seating arrangements or what color napkins would match the table centerpieces. She wanted to be with Brandon. He was unlike any man she'd ever known. Maybe it was the uncomplicated lifestyle he led, but being with him was just so...*easy*.

"Sure you can," he said. "It's *one* day."

"The gala is in three weeks. I have so much to do."

"But how much can you do on a Saturday? Take a drive with me instead."

"Where?"

"*Anywhere*. We could have a picnic."

She hadn't been on a picnic since…well, longer than she could remember. It was so tempting. But what she'd said about them wanting different things from life was true, and she didn't feel it was fair to lead him on, to make him believe this was something it wasn't. Something it could never be.

That didn't mean that they couldn't be friends.

"I'll go, but only if we both agree to keep this platonic."

"What if I want more?"

She stepped back, out of his arms. "Then we'll have to be business associates, and nothing more."

He considered that for several seconds, then shrugged and said, "Friends it is, then."

That was almost too easy. Either he was just saying it to appease her, or maybe he wasn't as attracted to her physically as she was to him. If he was, wouldn't he have put up at least a little bit of a fight?

What was wrong with her? She'd gotten exactly what she wanted, and she still wasn't happy! Maybe he took what she said to heart, and decided he wanted them to be friends.

And maybe she wanted to have her cake and eat it, too.

"So are you ready to go?" he asked.

"For a picnic?"

He nodded.

"Where?"

"I know a place. I think you'll like it."

She shouldn't go, but she wanted to. Badly. And how often did she do things just because? Try never.

Maybe, just for today, she could do something fun. "I'll get my shoes."

Five

On their way out of Vista del Mar—to parts still unknown—
Brandon pulled his truck into a parking spot in front of Bistro
by the Sea, a deli in the business district. It wasn't far from
Paige's office and she often picked up lunch there, or stopped
in for coffee.

"Sit tight," he said, getting out and heading inside. She
thought maybe he was picking up a soda, or more coffee.
Instead, he emerged several minutes later with an enormous
take-out bag. How had he managed that so fast? She could see
through the window that the line was long.

He'd gone outside to use the phone while she'd put on her
shoes. Had he been putting in a food order?

"What is that?" she asked as he got back in.

He handed it to her. "Lunch."

She took the bag, surprised by how heavy it was, and peeked
inside. He called this lunch? This was a feast! Gourmet sandwiches, salads and fresh fruit, plus a smaller bag of baked

goodies that had her mouth watering. There were even bottles of water and diet soda.

Being on a very strict budget, she knew the prices at the bistro. A spread like this must have cost him a small fortune!

"Brandon, you didn't have to do this," she said.

He shrugged as he started the engine, like it was no big deal. "You can't have a picnic without food."

"At least let me pay for my half," she said, reaching for her purse. It would be different if they were dating, but this was friendship, and it was only fair that they go dutch. Actually, since he bought dinner and all the drinks last night, she should be paying for lunch. "How much do I owe you?"

"This one is on me," he said, pulling back out into traffic.

"That's not fair. You bought last night. And with you working less, things have to be tight."

"My salary hasn't changed."

That was a surprise. "You must have a very generous boss."

"He is. He looks at it as an investment, I guess, since he's grooming me to be foreman."

She wondered if he would make substantially more as foreman, but she would never be so bold as to ask. How much he made was none of her business. Although she couldn't silence the nagging voice that said he was selling himself short. That he was an intelligent man capable of such greater things. Maybe he believed that at thirty years old, it was too late to change. Or maybe he really did love his work, and he was happy just the way things were. Who was she to dictate what was best for him? And why did it matter so much to her?

Because she liked him. A lot. Every time she looked over at him, her heart did a funny little flop in her chest. Maybe she wanted to try to mold him into someone who would fit her lifestyle, the persona she had created.

If that was true, something was very wrong with her.

He entered the I-8 going northeast and merged into traffic.

"You're not going to tell me where we're going?" she asked.
He just smiled.

"Do *you* even know where we're going?"

"Yep."

"Is it very far?"

"Twenty minutes, give or take."

He was very relaxed behind the wheel, letting the natural flow of traffic dictate his speed. Wherever they were going, it was clear he wasn't in a rush to get there. She, on the other hand, had the tendency to exceed the speed limit. Even if it meant staying only five minutes ahead of schedule. She was always in a rush to get where she was going, to finish one task so she could start the next. It was a perpetual cycle that never seemed to end. At times it could be exhausting. But it had been that way for so many years now, she didn't know how to change. How not to be in constant movement.

Maybe Brandon could teach her. Or maybe he wouldn't want her to change. Maybe he liked successful, professional women.

And maybe it didn't matter, she reminded herself, because they were just going to be friends.

"What was your fiancée like?" she asked him.

He looked a little taken aback by the question. "Where did that come from?"

"I was just curious. If you don't want to talk about it—"

"It's okay. You just caught me off guard." He drew in a deep breath and blew it out, shoulders tense. "Ashleigh. She was… ambitious. But not necessarily in a good way."

"How can ambition be a bad thing?"

"I guess it just depends on what you're ambitious about. She was the perfect woman for me, right up until the day I realized she wasn't."

"I'm not sure what you mean."

"She told me exactly what I wanted to hear, became exactly

who she thought I wanted her to be. What we had, it was an illusion. She said she never even loved me."

"Why would she do that? Why would she want to be married to someone she didn't love?"

"I'm sure she had her reasons."

Paige had the feeling there was more to it than he was telling her. That her reasons were something he preferred Paige not know. Or maybe he just didn't feel comfortable opening up to her. They had known each other less than twenty-four hours. Just because she'd experienced some sort of strange connection, it didn't mean he felt it, too.

"Thank God I figured it out before we made it to the altar," he said. "Although barely."

"When did you find out she was being unfaithful?"

"Two days before the wedding, when I caught them in the stable in a…*compromising* position."

She couldn't even imagine how horrible that must have been. And for the life of her she could not fathom why a woman with a fiancé so sweet and attractive would need anyone else. She had to remind herself that she didn't know Brandon very well. Maybe he had a dark side. Everyone had faults, right?

"How about you?" he asked. "Any serious relationships that have crashed and burned?"

"Not really. In high school I didn't have time for boyfriends. Besides, I didn't want to become one of *those* girls."

"*Those* girls?"

"From the wrong side of the tracks who ended up knocked up and married at sixteen."

"Things were that bad for you and your mom?"

"My parents got married right out of high school and my mom had no skills to speak of. Let's just say she didn't do the hottest job supporting us. After the life insurance money was gone, we lost our house and had to move into this crummy little trailer on the poor side of town. Once, it got so bad we had to live in a women's shelter for several weeks. It was the most humiliating experience of my life."

"Your mom never remarried?"

"No, thank God."

He glanced over at her. "That was a good thing?"

"She tended to hang around like-minded men."

"Other alcoholics, you mean?"

"Alcoholics, drug addicts. She wasn't terribly discerning. In fact, one of them was the reason we got evicted and had to stay in the shelter. My mom had the rent in her purse, and he stole it to buy drugs. She had to come up with first and last month's rent and a security deposit before we could move back in."

"I know what it feels like to be let down by a parent," he said.

"I like to think that it made me a stronger person. She may have screwed up a lot, but thanks to her, I know how to take care of myself."

He reached over and laid his hand over hers, giving it a squeeze, and she felt a corresponding squeeze in her heart. She almost wished he would keep holding her hand, but he let go and rested it back on the steering wheel.

"So, no serious boyfriends in high school," he said. "What about college?"

"There were a lot of first dates, and a few short-term relationships, but no one I ever fell madly in love with. There was one guy I dated in my junior year that got serious to the point that we were considering moving in together. But it just never happened. There was always some reason why it wasn't a good time. Then he graduated and took a job in Chicago. We tried to do the long-distance thing, but it didn't take long before we drifted apart."

"Were you in love with him?"

She shrugged. "I don't know. Maybe, in a way I was. I definitely loved him as a friend. But honestly, I don't think I've ever really been 'in love' with *anyone*." Which was why these intense feelings she was having for Brandon were so... unusual.

"And now you don't have time," he said.

"Not since I started my company. Besides, who in their right mind would want to date a woman who works eighty-hour weeks?"

He looked her way and grinned, and her heart did the funny little fluttery thing. "I guess it depends on the woman. And the man."

Well, she was still very single, meaning no man had found her so engaging he would tolerate her crazy schedule. Not that she'd been looking. And it wasn't very likely that the perfect man would just happen to come along. Which was okay. "For me, it's easier not to get involved right now. It's less complicated."

"And lonely, I'll bet."

"I don't have time to be lonely," she said, but that wasn't completely true. Occasionally, she missed just having someone to share things with, and the lack of physical intimacy sucked sometimes. Not that sex had ever been so fantastic that she felt it was something she couldn't live without.

Yet something told her it would be different with Brandon, and now, it seemed to be all she could think about.

"Does that mean you never want to get married?" Brandon asked Paige. Only out of curiosity, of course. After Ashleigh, he wasn't sure he would ever consider marriage again. Not for a long time, anyway.

"Someday, maybe," she said.

"What about kids?"

"I've never felt a burning need to have children. Not yet. I'm sure I will when the time is right."

"And when will that be?"

"When my business is established. When I formed the company I had a three-year plan, and year three just started. That's why the Hannah's Hope account came along at just the right time."

"And if it takes four years, or six?"

"I'm young, so there's no rush."

He would venture to guess that there were women out there who'd had similar plans, putting career over marriage and family, then suddenly found themselves pushing forty with no husband and no kids and a whole lot of regrets.

Not that he believed a woman needed those things to feel complete. Not all women. Besides, who was he to pass judgment?

He switched to the right lane and merged onto the I-15 going north. At the risk of offending her he asked, "How old are you, by the way?"

"I turned twenty-eight on January twenty-second."

He glanced over at her, to see if she was kidding. If maybe she'd looked in his file or something. "No way."

She looked at him funny. "Yes way."

"Your birthday is really January twenty-second?"

"It really is."

"So is mine."

Her brows rose. "Seriously?"

He laughed. "What are the odds, huh?"

"That is a little weird."

In his entire life he'd never met anyone with the same birthday. "Maybe it's fate."

"I don't think so."

"Why not?"

"Because I don't believe in fate. I believe a person is in control of their own destiny. My life is what I make of it. There are no cosmic forces determining what will and won't happen."

"I disagree," he said, which earned him a curious look. "Do you really think it was coincidence that two days before my wedding I just happened to come home from a business trip early, and just happened to notice the light on in the barn, and went to go check it? And just happened to catch Ashleigh—if you'll pardon the expression—with her pants down?" The exit he wanted was just up ahead on the right so he merged over.

"Your boss sends you on business trips?" she asked.

"Business trips?"

"You said you came back early from a business trip."

Damn, had he? He needed to be more careful. He was so comfortable with her, he was letting his guard down. "My boss was considering purchasing a few horses. I went with him to look at them."

"And you just happened to come back early?"

"Like I said, *fate*."

"You know, I think you're the first guy I've ever met who believes that kind of thing. Or the first one who would actually admit it."

He laughed. "Oh, no, have I emasculated myself? I thought women appreciated a man with a sensitive side."

"Maybe it's just that the men I've dated have always been more…*practical*."

"In other words, *boring*."

"Sometimes. But I prefer men who are safe."

"That's funny, last night you said you preferred men who were bad for you."

She bit her lip. "I did?"

"So which is it?" He pulled off the interstate onto the road leading to the park. "Good guys or bad guys?"

"Maybe it would be nice for a change to find someone who was a little of both." She looked out the passenger window and said, "Are we there?"

"Almost." He watched for the narrow access road that he'd discovered accidentally last month when he'd started coming here. It was so hidden by vegetation, he almost missed it. He took a left down what was barely more than a dirt path, and clearly posted as park maintenance access only. But he never had been one to follow the rules.

"Where are we?" Paige asked.

"Canyon Trail Park." They hit a dip in the road and almost got whiplash.

Paige grabbed the door. "Is this even a real road?"

He looked over at her and grinned. "Technically, no. It's more of an access road. I discovered it by accident."

"So, technically, we're not supposed to be here."

"*Technically,* no. But they haven't caught me yet."

"How often do you come here?"

"Every now and then when I'm in town. I'm not much of a city person. I need a place I can go to be alone."

He followed the road several hundred yards into a small, grassy clearing that was always devoid of cars, or any sign of other people. He parked in the shade of the trees and they climbed out of the truck.

She looked around, brow furrowed. "Maybe this is a stupid question, but what if one of us has to use the bathroom?"

"There's a public restroom about a quarter of a mile through there," he said, pointing to a small break in the underbrush. "Or if you don't want to walk that far, there are plenty of trees around. Although you'll want to watch out for poison ivy."

She shot him a look.

He shrugged. "The public restroom it is."

Brandon pulled out the thick wool blanket he kept behind the driver's seat and spread it on the grass in the shade of a tree.

Paige sat down, breathing in the fresh air. "It's really pretty here."

He lowered himself down beside her. "It's a little early for lunch."

"So what will we do until then?"

He shrugged. "Relax?"

She looked at him funny, like the concept was totally foreign to her. "I don't think I know how. Can't we take a hike or something? Or maybe we should discuss the gala and what will be expected of you."

It was going to be tough seducing her if she couldn't sit still for two minutes. "Or we could just sit here enjoying the mild weather."

"But why just sit here if we have things we could be accomplishing?"

Wow, she really didn't know how to relax. And somehow he didn't think forcing her was an option. But if she wanted to do something, then they would.

"In that case, I have an idea." He pushed himself to his feet and stuck out his hand to help her up. "Get up."

She slid her hand into his and he hoisted her to her feet. "What are we going to do?"

"I'm going to teach you to line dance."

Her eyes went wide. "You're joking, right?"

"Nope."

"Brandon, I can't."

"Last night you said you couldn't slow dance and you figured that out."

"This is different. Line dancing requires coordination, which I'm sure you noticed I am pathetically lacking."

"Once you learn the steps, it's just a matter of practicing. And out here you don't have to be worried about embarrassing yourself because there's no one to see you."

That didn't seem like much of a consolation for her.

"I'll teach you some simple steps first," he said. "When you get the hang of it we'll put on some music and try it out."

"How long have you got? Because that could take a really long time."

"That's fine," he said with a grin. "I have all day."

She still looked wary, so he added, "It's that or we just sit here relaxing. Your choice."

And if he had his way, dancing wasn't the only physical activity they would be getting today.

Six

It was obvious by Brandon's grin, that he wasn't going to let Paige off the hook. This was his idea of a fun day? But the thought of sitting here doing nothing made her edgy.

"Fine," she grumbled. "But for the record, I'm not happy about this."

"You'll do great," he said, looking pleased with himself, rubbing his hands together. "Okay, stand beside me and do exactly what I do."

He made it sound so easy, and it was clear, as he showed her the various steps, he was a really good dancer. And she really wasn't. She watched carefully when he demonstrated, but when she tried to copy him, she couldn't make her feet cooperate. It was as if she suffered from coordination dyslexia. Every time he went left, she went right—usually running into him—or if he stepped back, she stepped forward.

After twenty minutes or so, when they had managed to make no progress whatsoever and her last botched move landed her on his booted foot again, Brandon eyed her with suspicion and said, "Are you just messing with me, or are you *really* that uncoordinated?"

"I *really* am. It's hopeless."

He sighed, scratching his chin. "I think part of your problem is that you're trying *too* hard. You just need to relax."

"That's easy for you to say. You don't totally suck at this."

"I didn't come out of the womb knowing how to dance, you know. It took practice."

She seriously doubted it took even close to the amount of practice she would need. It wasn't helping that she kept getting distracted watching him move. She'd never met a man more blatantly male, yet he had an innate grace that was mesmerizing. She could only imagine how good he looked in the saddle.

Or naked. Not that she would ever find out.

"Now, watch my feet," he said, "And try to relax. This is supposed to be fun."

She could think of other "fun" things she would rather be doing with him, but only because he kept *touching* her. She never knew line dancing could be so intimate. A hand on her shoulder or the small of her back as he showed her a step, or the bump of his hip against hers when she inevitably did it wrong. Every time they made any sort of physical contact, it got her thinking about the kiss this morning, and how much she wanted to do it again. Brandon, on the other hand, seemed content honoring her request to keep things platonic. Which both relieved and annoyed her. She wanted to know that she wasn't suffering alone. That all the touching was as torturous for him as it was for her.

At around eleven-thirty he swabbed his forehead with his sleeve and said, "Phew! It's getting warm out here." Then he grabbed the hem of his shirt, pulled it up over his head and tossed it into the truck bed.

Oh, good Lord.

He was *perfect*. Tanned and muscular and just…just…*beau-*

tiful. He had a sprinkling of blond hair across his pecs, and a trail from his navel that disappeared under the waist of his jeans. She couldn't help imagining what it would feel like to touch it.

This was supposed to help her relax? Seriously? She could hardly *breathe.* And was that drool running down her chin?

She swiped it with the back of her hand just in case.

"Let's try that last part again," he said. "Only this time, stand behind me and watch my feet."

Good God, was he serious? That left her free to openly stare without him knowing. So much male perfection. Wide shoulders, a strong back. And his butt…

She sighed softly. Brandon was all man, and then some.

He looked back at her over his shoulder. "Are you following me?"

She dragged her gaze up to his face, feeling slightly faint. "Following you?"

"The steps. You're supposed to be doing them with me."

Had he been doing steps? She'd been too preoccupied staring at his ass to notice. "Sorry, I thought I was supposed to be watching."

"Put your hands on my shoulders."

Huh? He wanted her to *touch* him? "Why?"

"So you can move with me."

She swallowed hard and stepped up close, but he was so tall she couldn't reach higher than his upper back without plastering herself against him. His skin was warm and smooth and a little damp with sweat, and she could feel the muscles shift underneath as he moved. If having her hands on him had any effect on Brandon he didn't let it show, but it was sure as heck affecting *her.*

He stepped left, left, forward, forward, and she was doing okay. Right, right, back, back. She was doing it.

Left, left, forward—

She went forward and he went back and she slammed into

him again. She was so close she bumped her nose against his spine, and he was so solid she sort of...bounced off. She nearly landed on her butt in the grass. Brandon spun around and caught her by the arm. "You okay?"

"Yeah." This time. But that felt a lot like running into a tree trunk.

This was like the Three Stooges Dance Academy, minus one Stooge.

"Let's not do that again," she said.

"But you were doing pretty good for a minute."

"Yeah, but if I run into you like that again I might wind up with a concussion."

He folded his arms—which only accentuated how big they were—and gave her a look. "Maybe we should take a break."

"Could we, please?"

"Let's have lunch."

They settled down on the blanket. She sort of hoped he would put his shirt back on, but no such luck. So of course, she couldn't stop staring at his chest. She was so mesmerized at one point that when she tried to take a bite of her salad she missed her mouth and speared her lower lip with a plastic fork. She would have been perfectly content to sit there all afternoon staring, but Brandon was a man on a mission. As soon as they'd eaten, he dragged her back up for the second half of her lesson.

Even she had to admit that after another hour or so she started to get used to his bare chest, and the intoxicating scent of his aftershave. And as she followed his steps, she was running into him a lot less. Far from perfect, but she didn't feel quite so hopelessly inept. When she made it through an entire routine with only a few minor missteps, Brandon announced that it was time to try it to music. He rolled down the truck windows and turned on the stereo to a country-and-western station.

The main problem of dancing to the music was that it was

faster, and she started getting confused again. Within seconds she was right back where she started, ramming into him and stepping on his feet.

"Maybe the music was a bad idea," he finally said.

She blew out a frustrated breath. "Maybe the entire dancing idea was stupid. I suck."

"You do not suck. You're getting better."

"Can we please take another break? I'm exhausted."

"Five minutes."

She collapsed down on the blanket, lying flat on her back with her eyes closed. She felt him sit beside her.

She opened her eyes and looked up at him, intending to thank him for being patient with her, when she saw silhouetted against the sun, some enormous, creepy bug dive-bombing her head. She tried to roll out of the way but it came at her like a kamikaze pilot. It landed on her head and got tangled in her hair. She jolted up, batting it away.

"Get it out!" she screeched.

Brandon grabbed her shoulders to still her. "Calm down. I'll get it."

She had to fight not to squirm while he picked whatever it was from her hair.

"It's just a dragonfly," he said, holding it out so she could see. "They're actually supposed to be good luck."

Her cheeks flushed. She must have looked like a total moron thrashing around like that. "Sorry. Old habits."

He released it and it flew away. "You get bugs in your hair a lot?"

"Well, not anymore."

He was frowning, and she could see he was curious to know what she meant.

"Our trailer was infested with cockroaches. No matter how much I sprayed we couldn't get rid of them. I used to wake up at night with them crawling in my hair."

He didn't say a word. Maybe he wasn't sure what to say.

Instead, he put his arms around her, pulled her against him and just held her.

It was so unexpected, so exactly the right thing to do, tears sprang to her eyes and she had to fight to keep them from spilling over.

What the heck was wrong with her? She never got emotional. And she never cried. She was tough. A fighter.

But maybe she was tired of fighting, tired of being tough. Maybe she could be soft and vulnerable, just for a minute or two. Maybe it would be okay to let Brandon comfort her instead of pretending that her crummy childhood wasn't a big deal.

She leaned into him, tucking her face in the crook of his neck, breathing him in. He smelled like fresh air, sunshine and red-blooded male. She pulled back and looked up into his eyes. God, she could swim in them, they were so deep blue. She wanted to kiss him. To taste his lips and feel his beard tickling her. She wanted to run her fingers through his hair, her hands over his back and arms, feel all that lean muscle. In that instant, it seemed to be the only thing that mattered.

What was happening to her? How could she feel so deeply for someone she barely knew? For a man so completely wrong for her?

She reached up to slide her arms around his neck and he was already leaning in, anticipating the kiss, and when his lips brushed hers it was so sweet, so *perfect* she could have cried. She loved the softness of his lips, the taste of his mouth, the tickle of his whiskers. Who knew facial hair could feel so sexy? The slide of his tongue against hers was making her feel warm and soft inside. And once they started, she just couldn't seem to stop. She didn't *want* to.

Why hadn't they done this earlier? The moment they got here? Why fight it when it was just so…good?

She laid back against the blanket, pulling him down with her. She just wanted to kiss him and kiss him, keep kissing him until her lips blistered. She wanted to slide her hands all over him, but when she tried, he caught them in his own and held them still against his chest.

Without saying it, he was telling her that this wouldn't be going any further. Not here. And that was okay. She couldn't recall the last time she'd just made out with a man. Without the pressure of feeling the need to take it to the next level. She liked the feeling of excitement, the anticipation.

She wasn't sure how long they laid there kissing—it felt like hours—but suddenly she heard someone clear their throat, and she realized they were no longer alone.

She and Brandon looked up to find a park ranger standing a few yards away, arms folded across his chest, a stern look on his face.

Well, it was a really good thing they *hadn't* gotten too hot and heavy. Maybe that's exactly what Brandon had been thinking.

"Maybe you missed the signs, but where you came in isn't a public road," the ranger said, sounding irritated, as if he might have expected this from kids, but as adults they should have known better.

They probably should have.

"Sorry," Brandon said. "We'll leave."

The ranger nodded and walked back to the Jeep he'd apparently driven there in. She hadn't even heard him pull up.

"So, you've never gotten caught," she said under her breath as they got up.

He shrugged and answered back, "First time for everything."

She should probably feel guilty for breaking the rules. As long as she could recall she'd been the consummate good girl. But something about being bad felt a little…fun. It felt good to break from the mold.

Brandon grabbed the blanket, folded it and stuffed it behind the passenger's seat before he helped her in. She was a little disappointed when, on his way around the back, he grabbed his shirt and tugged it on.

He got in the truck, started the engine and swung around to head out the way they came, passing the ranger who was apparently waiting to be sure they really did leave.

They bumped along in silence for several minutes, then turned out onto the road.

"So, you kiss all your friends like that?" Brandon asked, wearing a smug smile, looking awfully pleased with himself, although she wasn't quite sure why.

"And if I said yes?"

The smile turned steamy. "Then I think I'm going to enjoy our friendship."

So was she.

"I figured the bare chest would do the trick," he said.

Do the trick? "What do you mean?"

"You just needed an extra little push to get the ball rolling."

Get the ball rolling? "Are you saying you brought me here to *seduce* me?"

He just grinned.

She wasn't sure if she should thank him, or bat him upside the head. Was it a sneaky move? Sure. But let's face it, she'd *wanted* him to seduce her, and that must have been pretty obvious when she made the first move. "I suppose keeping the relationship platonic wasn't totally realistic."

"It's tough to fight nature."

It certainly was. "That doesn't mean I'm looking for a committed relationship. I think we should keep it casual."

"Casual is good," he said.

It was a relief. Not that she'd anticipated him having a problem with that. What man in his right mind would turn down no-strings-attached sex? She was probably a dream come true.

"So, where to?" he asked, glancing her way, and his steamy

look said clearly where he wanted to go, and what he wanted to do when they got there.

And all she could think was *hell, yes*. Since sleeping with him at this point was inevitable, why put it off? "We could go back to my place."

"You're sure?"

She had never been so sure, never wanted anything more in her life. And if he was even half as good in bed as he kissed, she was in for a *very* good time. "Very sure."

"Just so long as you realize that means we're going to end up in bed."

"That's what I was hoping."

"Your place it is," he said, taking the on-ramp to the interstate.

She couldn't help noticing that he drove faster this time. Maybe he was worried that if it took too long, she might change her mind. That was not going to happen. It seemed as though for every minute that passed, her anticipation mounted, and by the time they exited the interstate, she was so excited she was practically squirming in her seat. But when they reached her neighborhood, instead of going straight to her apartment complex, he pulled into the lot of the convenience store just down the street.

They were thirty seconds from her apartment. Whatever he needed couldn't wait until later?

Her anxiety must have shown, because he said, "I have two condoms in my wallet, and I can tell you right now that isn't going to be enough."

Oh, boy. How many did he think they would be needing?

"I'll be right back," he said, shoving his door open, leaving the engine running.

Brandon was in and out of the store in thirty seconds flat. He climbed into the truck and tossed her the bag with his purchase. As he pulled out of the lot she couldn't resist peeking inside. It was a box of thirty-six, and they were extra-large.

Oh, boy.

As they pulled up outside her complex she realized that her car was still at work, but it would keep until later. Or morning.

"You should park in the lot behind the building," she said. "There's no parking on the street between 2:00 a.m. and 6:00 a.m."

The implication of her suggestion was not lost on him. He was grinning as he pulled into the lot and parked around back.

She stuffed the condoms in her purse and they both got out. Brandon took her hand as they walked to her door, and she was so excited, her heart was hammering in her chest.

Would he make love to her slow and sweet, or would he ravage her? The possibilities excited the hell out of her.

She unlocked the door and they stepped inside. She shut the door behind them and locked the deadbolt, so excited her hands were actually trembling.

She wondered if she should offer him a drink. If they were going to ease into this slowly, or just go for it. She didn't have to wait long to find out.

The second she turned to face him, Brandon looped an arm round her waist, hauled her against him and proceeded to kiss her socks off. Or would have, had she been wearing any.

She'd been with men who kissed too hard, too soft, too sloppy, but Brandon kissed just right. "I don't know where you learned to kiss like that," she said when they came up for air. "But you're really good at it."

"Marcy Hudson, eighth grade."

"Remind me to send her a thank-you note."

He grinned, dipping his head to take a taste of her neck, and the feel of his whiskers on her skin made her shiver.

"Is there anything besides kissing that you like to do with your friends?" he teased, easing her shirt aside so he could nibble her shoulder.

"Lots of things," she said, grabbing the hem of his shirt and tugging it up over his head. "But only my special friends."

He did the same to her, and when he got a look at her in her black lace bra he made a soft rumbly sound in his throat. He didn't seem to mind that she wasn't exactly blessed in the breast department.

He cupped her sides in his big, rough hands, sliding them upward, grazing her nipples with the pad of each thumb. Even through the lace the sensation was electric.

"Am I your special friend?" he asked.

"Why don't you take me to my bedroom and find out?"

Seven

Deep violet.

That was the color of Paige's eyes when she was aroused. A shade so unusual that if he hadn't known better he would swear they were contacts. Paige was truly unique. And it would seem, in some sort of rush to get him naked.

They barely made it into her bedroom before she was tugging at his belt, pulling at the button on his jeans. But Brandon had every intention of taking his time.

He tossed the box of condoms on to the bed—which surprisingly was unmade. He would have pegged her as the type of woman to keep a pristine house at all times. He caught her by the wrists and pinned her arms behind her back, tugging her against his chest, then he started to kiss her. Her lips, her throat, the ridge of her collarbone. He nipped her ear, her shoulder, finding that she seemed to like it when he used his teeth.

He wanted his mouth on every inch of her body. But all in good time. Since it had been a while for them both, he had every intention of making this last.

She tugged against his hands, her eyes shiny with lust, her lids heavy. "I want to touch you."

"You will." He dipped his head and pressed his lips to the swell just above the lace cup of her bra. Paige moaned softly and arched closer to his mouth. With his free hand he tugged the strap down and eased the cup off her breast. Her nipple was small and pink and pebbled to a hard point. He flicked it with his tongue and she sucked in a quiet breath, then he took her into his mouth and she groaned.

Her breasts were firm and soft. And so perfect that he couldn't imagine or want them any other way. There wasn't a single thing about her that he would change.

He sat on the edge of her mattress, putting her breasts perfectly level with his mouth, and tugged her between his legs. He let go of her wrists to unclasp her bra and slide it down her arms, then he pulled her in close to play with the tip of her other breast. She moaned as he sucked it in his mouth, sliding her hands across his shoulders, tunneling her fingers through his hair.

He kissed his way downward, until he reached the waist of her jeans. He could feel her anticipation as he unfastened the button, slowly pulled the zipper down. Through the V it created he could see the black lace of her panties. It was an odd quirk of his, but he felt a special fondness for a woman who went the extra mile and wore matching underwear. And more than being a breast or a thigh man, he liked to see said parts showcased in sexy lingerie. Black, red, purple—color didn't matter. But he had an affinity for lace.

Brandon hooked his thumbs in the belt loops of her jeans and eased them over her hips, down her legs. When they reached her feet she stepped out of them and kicked them away. Then he just looked at her. She had skin like delicate porcelain, and just the right curves for a woman her size. She was perfect.

He brushed his fingers across the lace crotch of her panties, watching her reaction. Her eyes rolled closed and she sank her nails into his shoulders. She was breathing faster and her chest had blushed deep red. It didn't take much to get her motor revving. Of course, he wasn't much better off. He was hard to the point of pain and aching for release, as if the last five months of celibacy were finally catching up with him.

He slipped his hand inside her panties, not surprised to find her slippery and ready. He stroked her and she shuddered. He did it again and she grabbed his arm.

"If you keep that up I'll come," she said.

"Isn't that the point?"

"I'm not ready."

He slipped a finger inside of her and she shuddered. "That's not what your body is saying."

"My body is ready, but *I'm* not. I want you to be inside of me. It just feels better that way."

It was tough to argue with logic like that, especially when he felt the same way. He wanted this to feel the best it could for the both of them.

He pulled his hand from her panties and she sank down to her knees in front of him to unfasten his jeans. He lifted his hips so she could pull them down, realizing, as his bare ass hit the cool sheets, that she'd taken his boxers along for the ride. She tugged them down and off his feet, then she wrapped her hand around the base of his erection and let out a soft, breathy sigh. "Wow."

"Too much?" he asked.

"Let's hope not," she said, then leaned forward and took him in her mouth. It was so not what he'd been expecting, she nearly did him in right then. He steeled himself against the sheer ecstasy of her hot mouth, and he'd just regained some semblance of control when, using her tongue, she concentrated on the small bundle of nerves just below the tip. Which just happened to be the number one most sensitive spot on his entire body. He was two seconds from a meltdown when he lifted her up off him and said, "I'm not ready yet, either."

She was wearing a sly smile that said she knew exactly what she was doing. She reached past him to grab the bag with the box of condoms and said, "Maybe now would be a good time to suit up."

She opened the box and pulled one out, tearing it open with her teeth.

"I think I should do the honors this time," he said. If she did it, he didn't honestly know if he could take it. He needed a minute to regroup. To think about nuns or baseball or something. "Why don't you lay down?"

She did as he asked, and when he was covered he joined her. Despite how sexy they were, it was clearly time to lose the panties. He slid them down, and as badly as he wanted to press her thighs apart, settle in and taste her, he stretched out beside her instead. She wrapped her arms around his neck and pulled him in for a kiss. A slow, deep one, that should have given his overactive libido a minute to cool down. Instead, all the writhing and moaning and rubbing against him that Paige was doing was only driving him closer to the edge. It was as if she was determined to make him embarrass himself. But he hadn't come before his partner since high school, and he'd be damned if he would let it happen tonight.

"You're going to have to slow down, sweetheart," he said.

She shook her head. "I can't. I want you now."

To prove she was serious she slid her hands down to cup his behind, simultaneously arching up to rub against him.

Holy hell, it was as if he'd unleashed some sort of wild animal. This was not the same woman he'd had to coax out for a drink, and drag onto the dance floor against her will. This woman was a purely sexual being. A wildcat. And she was so responsive to his touch, so easily aroused it made him want to beat his chest and roar.

He centered himself between her thighs, for fear that if he waited any longer he might lose ten small chunks of flesh from his backside. She looked so small, so petite, he began to worry that maybe he really would be too much for her. The last thing he wanted to do was hurt her. But she was whimpering and urging him on. She was, without question, ready for him.

He meant to take it slow, to give her time to adjust, but as he eased forward she arched up, impaling herself against him. He groaned as her slick walls closed around him like a fist, but Paige's wide-eyed gasp, her nails sinking into his flesh, stopped him cold. "Did I hurt you?"

She shook her head and said in a breathy but firm voice, *"Do not stop."*

Brandon pinned Paige's hands on either side of her head and thrust into her, swift and deep. *So* deep. She gasped in surprise as her blood fired and a feeling, like an electric charge, started in her womb and spiraled outward.

He eased back, his eyes locked on hers, and thrust into her again. The sensation was so intense, a shudder racked through her. She pushed against his hands. She wanted him closer, wanted to touch him, but he wouldn't let go. Though she had never been into bondage, or anything else that could be considered kinky, there was something exciting about being restrained.

He pulled back slowly, then thrust forward again, even harder this time. She cried out and arched against him.

He must have thought he hurt her, because he froze and said, "Too much?"

She shook her head and wrapped her legs around his hips. He loosened his grip on her hands and she clutched them tighter. "I like this."

The idea that she enjoyed being held down must have really turned him on, because things got a little crazy after that. And knowing how excited he was made it that much better. She tried to hold back, tried to make it last, which had never been a problem with any other man. But something about the way he moved, the slide of his skin against hers, the friction they created…it just felt *so* good. She could feel herself uncoiling, coming undone.

"Paige, look at me," he said. "I want to see your eyes when you come."

She gazed up into his eyes, and the ecstasy, the raw emotion in their blue depths wrecked her. Her body started to quake as pleasure seized hold. And whatever Brandon saw reflecting back in her eyes was his undoing. He groaned, his eyes pinned to hers as he climaxed, and she realized for the first time in her life what true intimacy really was. What it meant to connect with a man in the most profoundly personal way. And instead of tapering off, easing to the mellow pulses of afterglow, pleasure seized her again, taking her into ecstasy a second time, this one even more intense than the first. It was so overwhelming she actually lost herself for a minute. Couldn't see, couldn't hear, couldn't think. She could do nothing but feel.

At some point she must have closed her eyes, and when she opened them again, Brandon was grinning down at her.

"Did you just have a multiple orgasm?"

She nodded, her breath rasping out, her body as limp as an overcooked noodle.

"Is that a common occurrence for you?"

She shook her head. He had a way of doing amazing things to her. "First time."

His smile widened. "You're not just saying that to boost my ego?"

She laughed weakly. "I don't think your ego needs any help from me."

He kissed her, then rolled to sitting position at the edge of the bed. She heard him curse under his breath, then he shook his head and cursed again.

"What's wrong?" she asked.

"We have a breach."

A *breach?* "What kind of breach?"

"The condom. It tore."

Her heart skidded to an abrupt stop, then picked up double-time. "How?"

He shrugged and turned to look at her. "It's been known to happen. Is it a bad time for you?"

"Bad time?" Like, would 10:00 a.m. have been a better time for the birth control to fail?

"Is it a fertile time in your cycle?"

Oh. Good question. That wasn't something she thought much about, since up until now she hadn't been having sex with anyone. "I…I don't know."

"When was your last period?"

She must have looked surprised by the question because he said, "We've been about as intimate as two people can be. I think we're past using euphemisms."

Good point. "It was…" she figured the days in her head "…maybe a week ago."

"So we should be okay." His level of calm was both surprising and a little…disturbing. Most men in his position would be freaking out right about now.

"We should be fine," she said. "How is it you know so much about female reproduction?"

"I'm a rancher. I raise animals. It's the whole circle of life thing."

She hadn't though of that. "You're awfully…calm."

"What would be the point in getting upset? Why waste time worrying about something until you know you actually have something to worry about?"

That was a logical philosophy, and whether he realized it or not, Brandon was a truly unique man.

For a brief moment she tried to imagine what it would be like to have a baby with him. What the baby would look like. If it would have his dark blond hair and dimples. She wondered what kind of father he would be.

She realized what she was doing and shook the thought away. A baby with *Brandon?* What could she possibly be thinking? An affair was one thing, but to even consider a serious relationship was out of the question. They were way too different. And she was so not ready to even think about starting a family. Not when her business was at such a critical stage.

Maybe this affair wasn't such a hot idea after all. Not if she was going to let her emotions get the better of her. Maybe it would be best if they put an end to this before things got out of hand.

In theory it was a good idea, but then Brandon started kissing her again, and touching her, and of course she melted. She decided that she would make love to him one more time. Then she would tell him he had to leave, that they couldn't see each other anymore. But after they made love not one, but two more times, she was so exhausted she didn't have the energy to kick him out of bed. Besides, Brandon was a cuddler, and it had been a long time since she'd cuddled with a man. She fell asleep in his arms and woke the next morning to find him grinning down at her, his hair mussed from sleep. "We should get moving. I'm supposed to meet my mentor at eleven."

She smoothed down her hair, hoping she didn't look too beastly. "What time is it?"

"Ten after nine."

Ten after nine? She squinted at the clock to make sure he hadn't read it wrong. She never slept past six. Never. Now, to do it two days in a row. Of course, she didn't usually spend most of the night having sex, either. But it was over now, and she would have to tell him soon.

"I have to get to the office," she said.

"How 'bout a shower?"

"You can go first," she said.

That sly smile was back. "I was thinking the environmentally responsible thing to do would be to conserve water by showering together."

His smile was contagious. Maybe it wouldn't be so bad to

put off their talk another hour or so. "I'm all for water conservation."

"If you're really lucky," he said, grabbing another condom off the bedside table on their way to the bathroom, "I might even scrub your back."

Paige's car was still at work, so Brandon drove her to her office. They got a little carried away soaping each other up in the shower, and didn't pull into the lot until after ten. And by then, after several false starts of trying to bring up the subject of them not seeing each other again, she decided maybe a short affair wouldn't be such a bad thing. A week or two. Or maybe three. A month tops.

"Why don't you come in with me and we'll set up an appointment to go over everything you need to know for the award presentation," she said.

"Sure." He cut the engine and they both got out. He followed her to the door and waited while she unlocked it. She stepped inside, switching on the lights on her way to her office. It seemed surreal that she had met Brandon only two days ago, in this very room. Since then, it felt as if everything she knew about her life had been altered inexplicably. That she had changed somehow, and would never be the same person again. Or maybe she was making way too much of this. Maybe, after the affair was over, things would go back to being the way they were before, and she would forget what had been so wonderful about him. He would be just another guy she'd dated.

Although somehow she doubted it.

She slid in her chair and booted up her computer. Brandon sat on the corner of her desk beside her.

She typed in her password and opened her calendar. "When will you be in town?"

"I was thinking I might hang around for a few days instead of going home today."

She couldn't help wondering if that had anything to do

with her. She didn't want to be responsible for getting him into trouble with his boss. "Are you sure that's okay? Your boss won't mind?"

"He'll be fine with it. Trust me."

"Well then, how about 5:00 p.m. on Wednesday? I have to be at the tennis club anyway to look at the linens."

He frowned. "You want to meet at the tennis club?"

"That's where the gala will be held. Is that a problem."

He shook his head, but he looked hesitant. "No. No problem."

His uncertainty puzzled her. Maybe he was just worried about feeling out of place there, since it was an exclusive club that he wasn't a member of. Even she had to admit that it was a bit intimidating. Although, he didn't strike her as the type to care what other people thought.

She typed in the appointment. "Do you know how to get there?"

"I'm sure I can find it."

"Great. I'll meet you there at five." She closed her laptop and rose from her chair.

"I had better get going," he said, so she walked him to the front entrance. At the door he stopped and turned to her. "I had a good time last night."

"Me, too." Although "good" was a serious understatement. More like toe-curling, heart-throbbing, crazy wonderful.

"We'll have to do it again sometime," he said.

On a whim, and before she could consider the repercussions of her actions she said, "What are you doing Friday night?"

The question seemed to surprise him a little. "Nothing that I know of. Why?"

"I could make you dinner."

"I know you're busy right now. Are you sure you'll have time?"

If she didn't, she would make time. The only thing she was truly sure of at this point was that she wanted to see him again, wanted to spend the night with him and wake in his arms. And though Friday seemed like an awfully long time to wait, she couldn't let good sex—no, fantastic, *amazing* sex—sidetrack her from what was really important.

"I'm sure," she said.

He smiled. "Then I'd love to."

"Seven sound okay?"

"Seven works for me." He reached up, caressing her cheek with the backs of his fingers, and her knees actually went weak.

She could tell he didn't want to leave, but he said, "I should go now and let you get to work."

She rose up on her toes for a brief goodbye kiss. At least, it was *supposed* to be brief. But his lips felt so nice, and he smelled so good, the kiss just kept going and going, wrecking her common sense. His arms slid around her, drawing her against him, and she could feel that he was aroused. And God knows she was aroused, too.

She rubbed a hand over the bulge in the front of his jeans and he groaned.

She nibbled his lower lip and asked, "When do you have to meet your mentor?"

"Eleven."

It was only ten-fifteen. That left them plenty of time to have a little fun. "I don't know about you," she said, squeezing him through his jeans. "But I've never done it on a desk."

He looked down at her, his eyes shiny with arousal. "You're making it difficult for me to do the right thing."

"Yeah," she said with a smile as she tugged his shirt from the waist of his jeans, "But being bad feels pretty good."

Eight

Brandon sat on the bed in his hotel room Sunday, thinking about the last few days. It astounded him how, in the course of a weekend, his attitude about women and relationships had been altered.

He'd had more sex in the past two days with Paige, than the last three months of his relationship with Ashleigh. In hindsight, maybe the lack of intimacy should have tipped him off that something was amiss. He had just assumed they were in a phase, both busy with other things, and after the wedding their sexual desires would rekindle. And she *had* been busy with other things. Things like screwing someone else. And right under his nose. Maybe that was the most disturbing part of their split. Knowing that he'd been that gullible, that blind to what was going on under his own roof—or in some cases, his stable.

But when he looked back now, tried to recall what was so special about her that he'd wanted to marry her in the first place, he was having a tough time coming up with an answer.

At the time, it had seemed like the logical next step in their relationship—not the best reason for promising to commit the rest of his life to someone.

He'd loved Ashleigh in his own way, but his feelings for her came nowhere close to what, after only a few days, he was feeling for Paige. It wasn't love exactly. At least not any kind of love he'd ever felt. And he still had no clue where this relationship was headed, if he was ready for long-term. All he knew for sure was that after Ashleigh's betrayal, he didn't think he would ever be able to trust a woman again. Paige was different. She was unlike any woman he'd ever known.

She didn't care about wealth and social standing. She was more interested in making her own success than sponging off someone else's. And she appreciated him for the man on the inside. The real Brandon.

But how will she feel when she finds out you've been lying to her?

And even worse, if this gala was really so critical to her career, how was she going to react when he exposed Rafe in front of all those important people? Would they blame Brandon for wrecking the celebration, or somehow see it as her failure?

And if it was the latter, what was he supposed to do, just give up? Although at this point he wasn't sure he would have anything *to* expose. He'd spent all day online digging through county records and nonprofit regulations. Without physically looking at their books, he had turned that place inside out and he hadn't found a single thing yet that was the least bit fishy. And without access to the books, proving any deception was going to be tough. But he had an ace in the hole. A favor to call in. One he didn't want to use until he was at the point of desperation. Which he nearly was. With the gala less than three weeks away now, he was running out of time.

He was startled by a knock at his motel room door. Since no one knew he was staying there but his foreman and housekeeper, he rarely received visitors. Especially at nine-thirty at night.

He got out of bed, where he'd been doing his research, and walked to the door, peering through the curtain to see who it was.

Damn it!

It was Paige standing on the other side. How the hell had she known where to find him?

He looked around the room, taking stock of anything that might tip her off to the fact that he was not who he said he was. He gathered the papers off the bed and shoved them in the desk drawer, and because there was no way that she'd buy him owning a top-of-the-line laptop computer, he slammed it shut, dropped it in its case, and shoved it under the bed.

She knocked again and called his name.

He grabbed his wallet and shoved it in his back pocket. Not that he thought she would snoop, but it had his driver's license and he wasn't taking any chances.

He walked to the door and pulled it open, manufacturing a surprised look. "Hey, what are you doing here?"

"Is this a bad time? I knocked twice." She peered around him, like she expected to see someone else in there. A woman maybe?

He stepped to the side, so she could see that no one was there. "Sorry. I was on the phone. With my boss."

She frowned and took a step backward. "Oh, I'm sorry. Do you need to call him back? I can go."

"It's okay," he said. "Come in."

"Actually, I just came to give you this." She reached in her purse and pulled out the piece of crap watch that was a part of his disguise.

The fact that it was so cheap was the reason he wasn't worried when he couldn't remember where he'd left it. He'd figured it was probably at her apartment or her office.

He took it from her and said, "I wondered where that went."

"It was on my office floor. You took it off before we…" She trailed off, eyes shifting from him to somewhere over his left shoulder. Almost like she was afraid to look at him. "I just thought you might need it."

"Why don't you come in?" he said.

She shook her head. "I should get home."

There was something up with her. She was acting nervous. Edgy. Completely not like her. He folded his arms across his chest. "What's up, Paige?"

She blinked. "What do you mean?"

"Well, something is obviously upsetting you. You're uncomfortable, but I'm not sure why."

She bit her lip, gazing down at the faded, motel-green carpet. "It's…stupid."

"Talk to me."

"Coming here seemed like a good idea, but then I knocked on the door, and it took you so long, and I started to think that maybe you were…busy."

"With another woman."

She nodded. "And I got to thinking, what right do I have to just barge in on you like this? Unannounced. So, we had sex a couple of times. So what? It doesn't mean we have a relationship. That I can just show up."

He leaned in the doorway. "First, let me make one thing completely clear. There is no other woman. There hasn't been since my engagement ended, and there won't be, not as long as I'm seeing you. That's a promise. As for our relationship, or lack thereof, whether you like it or not, whether we intended it or not, we are in a relationship. Maybe it'll last a week, or a month, or fifty years. I don't know at this point. But what I do know is that what we have goes way beyond just sex."

Paige bit her lip and a small smile pulled at the corners of her mouth. She looked up at him, her eyes wide and deep blue.

And all he could think about was getting her out of her clothes and into his bed. He'd never intended on her ever coming here, but now he wanted her to stay.

"And as for barging in on me unannounced, you're welcome here anytime. Although I am a bit curious to know how you knew where 'here' was, since I don't recall telling you where I was staying."

Her cheeks flushed with embarrassment. "It was in the file I got from Hannah's Hope."

"So, are you going to come in?"

She licked her lips and nodded. "Just for a minute though."

Once he got his hands on her, it was going to take a lot longer than a minute.

"Excuse the mess," he said as she walked inside. He shut the door behind her. "I don't get many visitors, so I don't bother cleaning."

She set her purse down on the table by the window and picked up one of the hardback novels he'd forgotten to hide. He thought she might question his ability to attempt something so far above his reading level, but maybe she was afraid of offending him, because she put the book down without a word.

"Are you hungry?" he asked. "I have leftover pizza."

She shook her head. "I had a salad a couple hours ago."

"Something to drink? I've got beer and bottled water."

"No, thanks."

She still wasn't completely comfortable, and he had a pretty good idea why. "I think maybe we forgot something."

She turned to him, her brow furrowed. "What?"

He walked over to her, scooped her up into his arms and kissed her. She moaned softly and slid her arms around his neck, sinking into the kiss, her body soft and warm against his.

Yeah, that was better.

He kissed her lips, her neck, sliding his hands under her top.

"Brandon, I can't stay," she said, but she wasn't doing a darned thing to stop him. She didn't resist him when he pulled her shirt up over her head, or when he unfastened her jeans and pulled them down—in fact, she lifted her feet to help remove them. She didn't try to stop him when he lifted her and laid her back against the mattress, when he knelt beside her and eased her panties down, caressing her thighs and her stomach. She didn't tell him no when he pressed her thighs apart, lowered his head and took her in his mouth. And she sure as hell wasn't complaining when he brought her to an orgasm not once, but twice.

After they made love, and she lay draped over him, as he drifted off to sleep he figured it was a safe bet that she wasn't going anywhere until morning.

He wouldn't have it any other way.

Paige hadn't meant to fall asleep in Brandon's motel room, but when she woke, laying across his chest, it was 7:00 a.m. She had to get home, and ready for work, or she was going to be late—and she was never late. She tried to ease away without waking him, but the instant she moved, his arm slid around her, and when she tried to get up, he pulled her back down.

"Where do you think you're going?" he asked in a sleepy voice, his warm palm sliding up to cover her breast, and just like last night, she was incapable of telling him no. She hadn't meant for this to happen, to get so…involved. But Brandon was right. Like it or not, they did have a relationship. Sex, or more than sex…she didn't know. It was so good that, at this point, she didn't really care. Because she knew for a fact that anything this good, this sensationally smoking hot, was bound to burn itself out before things got too serious. It was inevitable.

It was over an hour later when she made it home to get ready for work. She didn't walk into work until nine-fifteen, which was unheard of for her. Cheryl was already sitting at her desk.

"This is a first for you," she said as Paige rushed through the door.

"Sorry, I got a late start." She walked into her office and set her case, with the work she had intended to do when she got home last night, on the desk. She was going to have to stay until midnight to catch up.

"You look like you didn't get a lot of sleep last night," Cheryl said.

"I was up late working," she lied. It was kinda like work, just the really fun, pleasurable kind.

Cheryl crossed her arms across her generous bosom. "You're a terrible liar. And it doesn't explain why you're glowing."

Glowing? "I am not."

"Yes, you are. You're lit up like a Christmas tree."

Cheryl planted both hands on Paige's desk. "I want to know what's going on. Have you been holding out on me? Seeing someone in secret?"

"Not exactly." Maybe she could tell her, without actually saying who.

"Is he married? Is that why you haven't mentioned him?"

"Of course not! And the reason I didn't tell you about him is that we just met Friday."

"Oh." Cheryl looked disappointed that it wasn't some torrid, forbidden affair. "When you didn't come back after the fitting with Mr. Dilson I should have figured you had a date, but…" Her eyes went wide and her mouth dropped open as she put the pieces together. "Oh, my God!" she shrieked. "Are you seeing *Brandon Dilson?*"

Paige could feel her cheeks turning red, which told Cheryl everything she needed to know. So much for keeping his name a secret.

"Oh, my God, you *are!* You bagged the hunky cowboy!"

"Don't get all excited about this. It's only an affair. It'll never amount to anything."

"Why, because he's not rich and successful? Who cares? He's *hot!*"

She cared. And it wasn't even that. She could get past Brandon not being rich and successful. Unfortunately, they wanted totally different things out of life, and one or the other would have to give up everything they cared about if they ever wanted to be together.

Cheryl sighed wistfully. "It was amazing, wasn't it? I mean, some guys you look at and you just know they'll be smokin' hot in bed. He has that look."

"Totally amazing doesn't even come close," she admitted, her cheeks flushing.

Cheryl plopped down in the chair. "God, I am so jealous. Do you know how long it's been since I met someone I wanted to sleep with, much less one who was better than totally amazing. In fact, I've never been with anyone who was better than pretty good. Men just don't appreciate a full-figured woman."

"You can't tell anyone."

She shrugged. "Who am I going to tell?"

"I don't know. But since technically he's a client, it's a serious conflict of interest."

"Paige, honey, you're planning a party. Not to diminish what you do, because you know I think you're a genius, but it's not like the fate of the world is resting on your decision to sleep with the guy. I seriously doubt anyone would care."

Paige knew she was right, but when it could be so easy to fall in love with Brandon, she was desperate for some handle on reality. Yes, he was honest and hardworking, but how could she put herself in a position to know even a shadow of the poverty she'd endured growing up? Brandon had made it pretty clear how much he loved his job, and that he had every intention of staying there. Which would leave her no choice but to leave her job to be with him. To fold her company before it had the chance to flourish.

She just couldn't do that. She couldn't take that sort of

chance, not when there was so much at stake. She couldn't imagine herself being content to live on a ranch foreman's salary. And it wasn't about the expensive clothes, because without her company she wouldn't need or want them. And it wasn't about having luxury vehicles, or pricey cell phones, or top-of-the-line home furnishings. She didn't have those things now, yet she was perfectly content.

What she couldn't live without was the financial security. She could never endure the constant feeling that any day the other shoe could fall, that there could be some sort of accident or tragedy that would wipe them out financially. What if one of them got sick? She could afford a good health plan through work. Was he even covered? And what if he was hurt and couldn't work any longer. She doubted he had a pension plan.

There were just so many variables. Too many questions.

"How does Brandon feel about this just being an affair?" Cheryl asked.

"How do you think he feels? He's a guy. Of course he wouldn't balk at no-strings-attached sex." But what was it he'd said about their relationship? He didn't know if it would last a week, or a month, or fifty years. She was sure he was just trying to make a point. That he didn't *really* expect this to last fifty years. They had agreed to keep it casual, right?

But they had also agreed to keep it platonic. And before that it was only supposed to be one drink. It was getting hard to keep track of what was going on when the rules kept changing. Maybe they needed to discuss this, just to be sure that they were on the same page, set some clear parameters.

"All of a sudden you don't look so sure about what you want," Cheryl said.

"I know exactly what I want." The question was, did Brandon?

Nine

Brandon sat in his truck in the parking lot of the Vista del Mar Beach and Tennis Club, dreading going inside.

When he left the city fifteen years ago, he never imagined he would see this place again. Nor had he any desire to. Too many memories. Too many he would rather forget. Now he didn't have much choice.

He was about to open the truck door when his cell phone rang. The ringtone indicated it was Clint Andersen, his foreman. He flipped his phone open. "What's up?"

"Hey, boss. Sorry to bother you, but I just got a call from that breeder in Texas. He's interested in coming to give those mares a second look. He'll be in the area Saturday morning."

"This Saturday?"

"Yup. Says he can stop in around 8:00 or 9:00 a.m. on his way back home. Sounds like a serious buyer to me."

Damn it. Brandon was supposed to have dinner with Paige Friday night. He would have to drive to the ranch instead to make sure the horses were ready, and get the paperwork in order. That would completely screw up their plans. But this was business, and he still had a responsibility to the ranch. He and Paige would have to reschedule. Maybe they could do it Saturday night instead. He could probably be back in Vista del Mar by midafternoon.

"Tell him to come by. I'll be there."

"Sure thing, boss."

He hung up and shoved his door open. He headed through the lot, past BMWs and Mercedes and pricey sports cars to the front entrance of the club. He hesitated there a moment, then opened the door. The interior still looked the same. It reeked of elegance and old money. During the summer months, when he wasn't at the ranch, this place had been like a second home to him. Every room, every corridor had been burned indelibly in his memory. And as tempted as he was to look around, he couldn't take the chance of someone recognizing him. He was almost positive that with his hat on, and his sunglasses hiding his eyes, no one would connect him with the fifteen-year-old boy who used to hang out there. Besides, what were the odds he would run into anyone he knew? The staff had to be different by now.

Get in, get it done and get out.

A group of women in tennis whites stood outside the lounge, eyeing him curiously. None of them looked familiar, but he wasn't taking any chances. He pulled the brim of his hat low over his eyes and headed down the corridor to the banquet hall. Down a hall to his left were the men's locker rooms, and the door leading to the indoor-outdoor pool. He could even smell a hint of chlorine. It brought back memories of endless hours spent swimming with his friends, with Emma always there pestering them. There had been swimming lessons in the Olympic-size indoor pool, and splashing under the rock waterfall outside in warmer weather. While his mother sat in the bar drinking away her resentment for Brandon's father, of course. Although occasionally she would indulge in a game or two of tennis with Brandon and Emma.

When he was older he hung out on the beach, swimming in the cove with his buddies and kissing girls at the base of Busted Bluff, in the privacy of the rocks. He used to think he was pretty hot stuff. That changed when he was fourteen, the day his world came apart.

He'd come home from the club to discover his parents fighting. Flinging hateful words and accusations. Which wasn't all that unusual, but this one had been worse than most. He actually began to think that maybe this was it, the fight that would drive that final wedge between them. And in a way he'd wished it would. Then his father would move out and his mother would finally be happy. She would stop anesthetizing the pain with alcohol and pills.

Eventually his father had stormed out, on the pretext of attending a late business dinner, but probably to see his latest mistress, even though he vehemently denied having one. But Brandon had heard the rumors, overheard people talking at the club and the factory.

Brandon gave his mom a while to calm down, because he knew she didn't like him to see her crying, then he went to look for her and found her unconscious on her bedroom floor. He'd called 911, and rode along in the ambulance while they had tried to revive her, but it had been too late.

If only he had checked on her sooner, he might have been able to save her. If only his father had learned to keep it in his pants, she wouldn't have been so miserable that she believed the only way out was to take her own life.

If only.

Brandon had stopped coming to the club after that. He couldn't stand the whispers and conjecture. Because even though it had been ruled an accident, everyone knew Denise Worth had committed suicide. Knew she was nutty enough to do it.

He shook away the memory. Now was not the time to be dredging up the past. Not when he had an appointment to keep. An appointment with a woman who, for the first time in his life, saw him for who he really was. Not a name or a bankroll. Just a man.

As he walked through the open banquet-room door he bumped shoulders with a man who was on his way out, the last person he wanted to meet face-to-face.

Rafe Cameron.

Damn it! So much for not running into someone he knew.

"Sorry," Brandon mumbled, keeping his head low, hoping Rafe would just keep going.

Instead, he stopped and turned. "Excuse me."

Did Rafe recognize him? It had been years since Brandon had seen anyone associated with the factory. Had he come this far, invested four months of his life, only to blow it now?

Brandon stopped and turned. Rafe gave him the once-over, eyes narrowed with obvious distaste, and said, "This is a *private* club."

Brandon heaved a silent breath of relief. He didn't recognize Brandon, he just didn't want a nonmember—a man he obviously considered beneath him—roaming the halls, making trouble. As if his presence alone might stain the club's good name.

Wouldn't he be surprised to learn that because of his father, Brandon, too, was considered a lifetime member. He recalled a time when Rafe hadn't been welcome in the club. When he was nothing but the son of factory employees. Employees who had been fired for fraternizing with each other. But now, dressed in a silk suit and Italian leather shoes, Rafe was the antithesis of his former self. A new man.

His hatred for Rafe, for everything he represented, clawed Brandon from the inside out.

"Brandon, you made it," he heard Paige say, and turned to see her walking toward them from the opposite side of the banquet room. She was wearing a designer suit, mountainously high heels and her hair was swept up in a twist. And despite his less than stellar mood, Brandon couldn't help grinning a little.

"Ms. Adams, you know this man?" Rafe asked.

"Mr. Cameron, this is Brandon Dilson. He's been working with one of the mentors and he'll be the recipient of the outstanding achievement award at the gala. Brandon, this is Rafe Cameron, the founder of Hannah's Hope."

"Mr. Dilson, congratulations on your success," Rafe said, without an apology, or a single note of regret for his initial suspicions. Arrogant ass.

Brandon had no choice but to accept his outstretched hand, masking his distaste with a polite smile. "Good to meet you."

Rafe turned to Paige. "I forgot to ask, where are you planning to set up the stage."

She turned and pointed to the opposite side of the room. "Over there will be best, I think. It's what the club recommended."

While her back was turned, Brandon caught Rafe red-handed staring at Paige's ass. His hackles rose and it took every bit of restraint he possessed not to punch the cocky son of a bitch in the jaw. Immature as it was, he had to fight the temptation to grab Paige and kiss her right there in front of Rafe, brand her as his own so the other man knew she was off-limits.

Which, he was sure, would piss her off to no end because as far as she was concerned, she wasn't Brandon's to claim. But it gave Brandon a childish satisfaction that, while Rafe clearly considered himself the better man, Brandon was the one who had spent practically an entire weekend in bed with her.

One of life's little ironies.

Paige turned back to Rafe and said, "If you had a different arrangement in mind, I'm sure we can work something out with the staff."

"That's not necessary."

"Are you sure? It isn't a problem."

He flashed her a charming smile. "You're the expert. I trust your judgment."

So why had he even asked? Was it simply to pull rank and make it clear to Brandon that he was in charge? Like Brandon gave a crap.

Rafe looked at his watch—a fifty-thousand-dollar platinum, diamond-studded Blancpain—and said, "I have a meeting to catch. It was good to see you again Ms. Adams, and a pleasure to meet you, Mr. Dilson."

Brandon couldn't say the same. He nodded politely and stuffed his hands in his pockets, so he wouldn't have to shake Rafe's hand again.

"So, that's your boss?" he asked Paige when he was gone.

"Technically, no," she said. "*I'm* my boss. But if you're talking about my client, Hannah's Hope, then I guess he would be considered the one in charge. Although typically I deal with Ana Rodriguez. Why do you ask?"

"He just seemed like kind of a jerk."

Her brow crinkled. "Why would you say that?"

He shrugged. "Just my opinion."

"I thought you gave everyone the benefit of the doubt."

He had told her that, hadn't he? But he already knew exactly who Rafe Cameron was. He just couldn't tell her that.

"When you turned around he was staring at your ass," he said. "It was unprofessional and tacky."

A smile curled her lips. "Brandon, are you jealous?"

"No." He certainly hadn't meant to give her that impression. Of course, his instant defensiveness did indicate a certain level of protectiveness for Paige. And okay, maybe some jealousy. He grinned and added, "Well, maybe just a little."

"Well, if it will make you feel better, Rafe Cameron isn't my type at all. He's too…stuffy." She leaned close, and lowered her voice. "I prefer bad boys, remember?"

She was close enough that he caught a whiff of her perfume. And if they hadn't been in a public place, she would already be in his arms. And they would both be in various stages of undress.

All in good time.

"Mr. Cameron is definitely thorough," she said. "He just spent the last two hours going over the plans for the gala down to the finest detail."

"Was he satisfied with what you've done?"

"For the most part. He had a few minor changes he wanted to make to the menu. And he must have mentioned a dozen times how important it is that this go off without a hitch. Ward Miller will be announcing that his foundation is making another substantial donation, so he wants everything to be perfect."

He wondered how Rafe would feel if he knew that the unveiling of Brandon's deception was on the agenda, and he could hardly wait to see Rafe's face when he exposed him in front of all those important people.

It wouldn't be long before Brandon knew exactly what Rafe was up to. He had a friend from college who was creative about accessing information via cyberspace, and if all went well, Brandon would have copies of the foundation's financial files by the end of the week. He would pass those on to a forensic accountant acquaintance who would comb the files for anything even slightly suspicious. Anything to warrant a formal investigation.

It wouldn't be cheap, and he wasn't exactly comfortable stepping outside of the law, but this was bigger than him. Any repercussions would be worth it when he brought Rafe down.

What he was beginning to dread was that in the process, he could very well be bringing Paige down with him. But how much was he willing to sacrifice for a short-term affair? There was a good chance no one would hold her personally responsible for an element of the party that was clearly out of her control.

That didn't mean she would resent him any less when she learned the truth. Or maybe with her own complicated past, she would understand his need to rectify his mistakes. And surely she would appreciate his efforts to save the city, and the livelihood of everyone who depended on the factory to put food on the table. If the rumors were true, and Rafe planned to break Worth Industries apart and sell the pieces, the blow to the local economy would be detrimental. Brandon had to do something, and he had to act soon. If he proved to the people of the city that Hannah's Hope was a fraud, maybe they would stand up against Rafe and fight to save the plant. Not only could the city be saved, but his family would be vindicated.

He didn't want to hurt Paige, but this was bigger than him. Bigger than both of them. He would just have to make her understand that.

"So," Paige said, turning to the bank of windows overlooking the ocean. "What do you think of the room? Won't it be perfect?"

"Nice view," he said. The last time he was here it was for the high school homecoming dance his sophomore year. That had been his last year at the Bay Academy. The following fall his father had shipped him to the east coast. Had Brandon been difficult, bordering on juvenile delinquent even? Hell, yeah. He'd resented his father for driving his mother to suicide, and he had given him one hell of a hard time.

He had been screaming for attention, but his father didn't even try to reach out to him. He only had time for his princess, Emma. In fact, she was cited as the reason Brandon was being sent away. Their father was worried that Brandon's behavior would rub off on her.

Brandon barely had time to grieve the loss of his mother before he was ripped away from everything familiar and forced to make all new friends. Which, before then, had always come easy to him. But it had been a rough adjustment. It was the reason he hadn't been back to visit his family in all these years. And since he'd taken over the ranch eight years ago, neither his sister or father had even bothered to visit. They hadn't even known about his engagement, and they weren't invited to the wedding. Unfortunately, at the gala, he would be forced to see them both, and he wasn't looking forward to it.

He wished he could talk to Paige, tell her what was on his mind. He normally wasn't one to discuss his feelings, but he knew she would understand what he was going through. After all, she had been abandoned by her mother. She may have physically been around, but she had checked out of Paige's life the minute she chose a bottle of booze over her own daughter.

If Brandon ever had kids he would do things differently. He would learn from his parents' mistakes. His children and their well-being would be his number-one priority. But first he had to find someone he would want to have children with. Someone he could spend the rest of his life with. Could that woman be Paige?

"Before we get started, why don't we take a walk outside," she said, gesturing toward the French doors that, if memory served, opened up onto a slate portico overlooking the cove.

He nodded and followed her outside. The breeze blowing in off the water had a chill and the cove was more or less deserted. A few kids played in the sand under the watchful eyes of young women who were more likely nannies than parents. But it was far too cold for swimming.

The wind whipped a few strands of Paige's hair loose and she tucked it back behind her ears.

"You know, every time I see your hair like that, all I can think about is messing it up," he said.

"I sort of wanted to talk to you about that," she said, then added, "Not my hair, obviously, but our…relationship."

"Okay."

"I know we already discussed it, but I just wanted to… clarify. We are keeping this casual. Right?"

So, they were back to this again. She was nothing if not

thorough. He folded his arms across his chest. "That was the plan."

She looked relieved. "Okay, good. I just…I wasn't sure if I'd made that clear enough."

"No, you were pretty clear the first time." Ironic since in most of his relationships he was the one saying they needed to keep it casual. He'd been with Ashleigh for a year before he would even consider a commitment. And now that he'd found a woman who finally saw him for who he really was, someone he might want to get more serious with, *she* was the one with commitment issues.

Not that he was ready to commit to anything just yet. But he didn't want to exclude the possibility, either. And when the day came that he wanted more, he didn't doubt he could make Paige see things his way. Because while she acted all independent and tough, she was marshmallowy-soft on the inside.

"Doesn't make much sense to get serious when I'm leaving town the day after the gala," he said. Which gave him exactly two and a half weeks to decide exactly where this relationship was going.

"So let's just have fun until then," she said.

He grinned. "I like fun, especially if it's the kind we have without our clothes on."

Her cheeks flushed. "I've been thinking about you a lot the past couple days."

"Me, too." He took a step closer and she licked her lips, as if she was anticipating a kiss. Then she took a step back, shaking her head.

"We can't do this here."

He moved closer. "Do what?"

She moved back. "Whatever it is you're thinking of doing. Kissing me, touching me."

"Sliding my hand up your thigh and under your skirt…"

"Exactly."

"I wonder if you're wearing a garter, like the other day."

She narrowed her eyes at him. "How did you know I was wearing a garter?"

"Your skirt slid up when you got in my truck. I saw the top of your stocking. And coincidentally, that just happens to be one of my all-time-favorite articles of clothing."

There was mischief in her eyes, and heat, as if she knew she was playing with fire, but just couldn't resist. "I might be wearing one."

"I think I need to look and see."

Her eyes widened a little. "Not here."

"There isn't anyone around," he said, walking around to stand behind her, so his body was blocking the view from the banquet room windows. "Who would see?"

"Brandon, don't," she said, but she wasn't moving away, and he could tell by her breathing—and the blush in her cheeks— that she was getting excited. A closet exhibitionist, maybe?

"No one will see." He pulled her closer, so that her back was against his chest, and peered over her shoulder. He hooked a finger under the hem of her skirt then slowly eased it up her thigh, grazing her stocking-clad skin.

"Brandon, please," she pleaded in a breathy voice, but he knew she didn't want him to stop. She liked it. If she didn't, she would have pulled away by now.

He dipped his head and pressed a kiss to her neck and her head sank to one side. He watched as the top of her stocking came into view, then the strap of a lacy red garter.

God damn.

He should have stopped there, but instead he slipped his hand between her thighs, against her warm skin, and a gasp slipped from between her lips. He slid his hand upward. He could feel her trembling, see her breath coming faster. Then his fingers brushed the crotch of her panties and she moaned. She squeezed her thighs together, as if to hold him there.

He had every intention of sliding his fingers under the lacy fabric, but he heard voices, and the sound of people approaching from the path that wound around the building from the parking lot.

He pried his hand from between her thighs and backed away just as two women rounded the corner.

Paige swung around to face him, simultaneously straightening her skirt, saying in a husky voice, loud enough for the women to hear. "Mr. Dilson, shall we go back inside?"

Brandon grinned. Her cheeks were bright pink, her eyes a vivid shade of violet. He'd just rattled the hell out of her. "Sure thing, Miz Adams."

He stepped past her to open the door, and as they stepped inside she hissed, "I can't believe I just let you do that. What is wrong with me?"

"Did it feel good?"

"God, yes."

"Let's face it, sweetheart, deep down, you're a bad girl. So bad that you want me to take you somewhere I can get you naked. After I get a good look at the garter, that is."

He could tell she wanted to say yes, but she resisted. He'd have been shocked if she hadn't, and truthfully, he enjoyed the challenge of bending her to his will.

"But we have an appointment. We're supposed to be getting you ready for the gala. Time is running out."

"I'll bet, if you got creative, you could teach me everything I need to know in the comfort of your bedroom."

"I *can't.*"

"You mean you won't."

"I have things to do."

He reached up to caress her cheek. It was flushed pink and warm to the touch. He rubbed her earlobe between his fingers and she closed her eyes. "Think about how much fun we could have."

She looked across the room, where apparently she'd planned to work with him, then over to the door. Then she sighed and said, "You are so bad for me."

He grinned. "And you love it."

Her smile said she did. "Let me grab my briefcase, then let's get out of here."

Ten

Paige didn't know how it was possible, but sex with Brandon just kept getting better and better.

When they stepped inside her apartment, she'd barely gotten the door closed before they were kissing and tearing at each others clothes. He seemed to instinctively know exactly what to do to drive her crazy. He managed to find every erogenous zone on her body—including a few that she hadn't even known were there—and, boy, did he know how to use them. He practically worshipped her body, and he never took his own pleasure until she had been thoroughly satisfied first. Usually twice. Of course, she was so turned on by everything he did, it didn't take much to have her writhing in ecstasy.

After they made love, they rehearsed for the gala, which Brandon did naked in her bedroom, bless him. That led to them making love a second time. Afterward, Paige should have gotten dressed and gone back to the office to finish up the preparations for a wedding the following weekend. Instead they collapsed in an exhausted, sweaty tangle on her bed and cuddled.

"So, what sounds better for dinner Friday?" she asked him. She lay draped across his chest, listening to the thump-thump of his heart against her ear. "I can do Italian or Mexican."

"I wanted to talk to you about that," he said. "I'm going to have to cancel."

The crushing disappointment she felt surprised her, but she tried not to let it show. This was just a casual relationship. A broken date should *not* be that big of a deal. "Oh, well, that's okay."

"It's not that I don't want to come over. But I have to be at the ranch early Saturday morning to meet with a breeder. It could be a pretty substantial sale."

"Isn't that something your boss would do?"

"Normally he would, but he'll be out of town for the weekend and he wants me to be there in his place."

"That's good, right? I mean, he trusts you to handle it."

"Yeah, but I hate breaking our date. I thought maybe we could try for Saturday, instead. Unless…"

She glanced up, saw that he had a thoughtful look on his face. She rose up on her elbow. "Unless what?"

"You could…come with me."

"To the ranch?"

"We could drive up Friday after work and come home early Sunday morning. You would only lose one working day."

Well, losing one day certainly wouldn't be detrimental. Since her meeting with Mr. Cameron went so well earlier, she was actually almost ahead of schedule. "Where would I sleep?"

He grinned. "Not in the bunkhouse with the men, if that's what you're thinking."

She gave him a playful poke. "I was thinking more along the lines of a hotel."

"My boss will be okay with us using one of the spare bedrooms in the main house. And there's a lot to do up there. We could go hiking up to the river, and horseback riding. And I could take you into town. Being from a small town, I think you would like Wild Ridge."

It was an appealing offer. Of course, he could suggest they take a trip into the barren desert and as long as she was with him, she would probably say yes. "You're sure your boss wouldn't mind?"

"Very sure."

There was something in his eyes that said this meant a great deal to him. And she couldn't deny that she was curious to see where he lived. To see him in his natural environment. Though her first instinct, when faced with an opportunity that would take her away from work was to always say no, she really *wanted* to go. And it was only *one* day. One of only seventeen or so that they had left together. She wanted to spend as much time with Brandon as she could.

"Of course I'll come," she said. "I'd love to see the ranch."

Brandon grinned. She could see she'd made him happy, and that made her happy.

"When can you be ready Friday?" he asked.

"Why don't you pick me up around six? How should I pack?"

"Casual. Warm days, chilly nights."

"So I should bring my flannel pajamas?"

"Like I'm going to let you wear any pajamas," he said, pulling her to him for a long, deep kiss. One that just kept going and going. Then he started touching her, and though she really needed to get a good night's rest, she just couldn't seem to tell him no. But this time when he made love to her it was slow and tender, and so sweet that when he cut their cuddling short and rolled out of bed to get dressed, she couldn't bear to see him go. Tossing her good sense right out the window, she grabbed his hand and pulled him back to bed. "It's late. You might as well just stay the night."

"Are you sure?" he asked.

She could see that while he didn't want to go, he was more than willing to leave if that's what she wanted. For some crazy reason, that made her want him to stay even more. Besides, they only had seventeen days left together.

"I'm sure." She tugged on his hand and he slipped back under the covers.

As she lay there later that night, listening to his slow, even breaths as he slept, feeling the warmth of his body as he lay wrapped around her, she experienced a sense of inner peace, a *happiness,* that was completely unfamiliar to her. A soul-deep need to be close to him that she'd never felt with a man.

Could this be what it felt like to fall in love? Was it even possible to fall in love with someone in less than a week?

If it was love, she had less than three weeks to get over it. Because even if she wanted more from this relationship, Brandon clearly didn't. After what his fiancée had done to him, who could blame him? And even if he ever did consider marriage again, she doubted he would want to be married to someone like her. They were too different. That didn't mean they couldn't have fun together in the meantime. Especially the naked kind.

Even if that meant a little heartache when it was over.

It was official, Brandon had completely lost his mind.

What the hell had he been thinking, asking Paige to come with him to the ranch? Clearly he *hadn't* been thinking. Because her being there was a logistical *nightmare.*

"Are you out of your mind?" his housekeeper, Ellie, asked him when he called Thursday afternoon to tell her they would be having a guest. She was one of only two people who knew what he was really doing in Vista Del Mar, and the chance he was taking bringing Paige to the ranch.

"Yeah, I probably am," he told her. But the offer had just sort of popped out before he'd had time to consider the repercussions, and once they were out there, there was no taking them back. Especially not when he saw how excited Paige looked. And weirdly enough, he really *wanted* to bring her there. In the past week they'd spent all their time together on her turf. He wanted to share some part of his own life with her.

It would be nice if he could do it without blowing his cover.

"Can you see that the spare room next to mine is aired out, and fresh sheets are put on the bed?" he asked Ellie. "We'll be staying there."

"You're not going to sleep in your room?"

"You really think she'll believe that not only is my boss willing to let me bring a guest in the house, but he would let us shack up in his bedroom?"

"Good point."

He could hear the clang of pots in the background. He could picture her in her apron at the stove, fixing supper for the men. She'd been a permanent fixture in the house since before he was born. "I'll also need you to go through the house and put away anything that has my name on it, or photos with me in them."

"That shouldn't take long. The only pictures you had up were of you and the hussy, and I think you burned all those."

Certainly not something he was proud of, but Ashleigh had been pretty big on capturing their life in print, so it had made one hell of a bonfire. And Ellie had been right there with matches and lighter fluid, egging him on. She had never cared much for Ashleigh. She always thought she was spoiled and selfish. And Ashleigh had nagged Brandon incessantly to fire Ellie, claiming that she always gave her the evil eye, and treated her like an outsider. Since the minute Brandon kicked her cheating behind out the door, Ellie referred to her only as *the hussy*.

Ellie was a tiny thing—no more than one hundred pounds soaking wet—but what she lacked in size, she made up for in attitude. She'd been like a mother to him since he'd moved back to the ranch. And there were times when she treated him more like an adolescent than an employer, but he loved her to death.

"What are you going to do about the men?" she asked.

"Clint is talking to them." He was the only other person who knew of Brandon's plans.

"Someone is bound to slip and call you boss."

"Paige thinks I'm being promoted to foreman as soon as I move back to the ranch. I can make something up about the men calling the foreman boss."

"But they would *never* do that."

"Yeah, but she doesn't know that. She doesn't know anything about ranching. As long as no one uses my last name I should be okay."

"I still think you're playing with fire. Which means you must be awfully fond of this woman. You've known her what, a week?"

"Not even."

"It took you three months to bring the hussy here."

A fact that was not lost on him. "She's different than any of the women I've dated before. She thinks I'm an uneducated ranch hand and that doesn't seem to matter to her. And when it comes to dysfunctional childhoods, we have a lot in common. I just…I like her. I feel good when I'm with her. And the sex…"

"I get the point!" she shouted, and Brandon laughed. That's what she got for being nosy.

"I guess she's going to be pretty surprised when she learns the truth about you."

"I imagine she will be." What would be even more surprising to her was the fact that he would risk destroying her professional reputation to expose Rafe. But he didn't have a choice. Although, despite how much he wanted to bury the son of a bitch, lately Brandon had actually begun to hope that he *didn't* find anything to discredit Hannah's Hope. There were so many people who would be hurt if his suspicions were true. Ana, who ran the foundation, and even his sister, Emma, who sat on the board. Not to mention all the volunteers whose only motivation was to help people.

But wouldn't they be hurt eventually, anyway? If the foundation was a fraud, the truth would come out someday. Better to expose Rafe now rather than later.

"It's real possible she'll be angry with you."

"Yeah, it's possible." In fact, it was an inevitability. The question was *how* angry would she be?

"If you care that much about her, is it really worth risking that?"

"I don't have a choice, Ellie. I have to do this. For the people of Vista del Mar."

"Are you sure you're doing it for them? I know that you feel that you failed your father. Are you trying to ease your own guilt?"

A month ago, the answer to that question had been clear. Now he wasn't so sure.

Eleven

Paige knew absolutely nothing about the ranching business, but it was clear, as Brandon pulled the truck up the road to the Copper Run, that this was no small operation. Tucked into a grassy valley in the San Bernardino Mountains, the sprawling log-cabin-style home, barn and stables weren't at all what she'd expected.

She was ashamed to admit that not only had she expected a much smaller business, but she had pictured it as being more rustic and modest. But not only was the house practically a mansion, the stables were huge and everything looked modern and well-maintained.

Vast pastures enclosed by white fences stretched as far as the eye could see, and roaming about were more horses than she could count. Beautiful animals in a wide range of colors and sizes. The valley itself stretched at least half a mile wide, surrounded on three sides by rocky slopes. The view as they pulled up to the house, with the sun setting over the snowy peaks, was utterly breathtaking.

No wonder Brandon didn't want to leave. She had been here a sum total of one minute, and already she regretted her trip would be so short. There were probably a million things to see and explore.

Brandon rolled to a stop in front of the house, at the base of a wraparound porch. Flower beds, in full bloom with tulips, irises and daffodils, bordered the entire length, and potted trailing flowers hung from the porch roof. The effect was warm and welcoming.

They got out of the truck and Paige filled her lungs with clean, crisp mountain air. And just like that, the stress of all the work she had waiting for her back home seemed to melt away.

"So, what do you think?" Brandon asked.

"It's *beautiful*." Several men dressed in cowboy gear stood by the largest of the stables, watching Brandon and Paige. They were obviously talking about them, but were too far away for Paige to hear what was being said. "How big is the ranch?"

"Over one thousand acres."

"That's a lot of land."

"Yes, ma'am."

She glared at the *ma'am* reference and he grinned. "And you'll be in charge of all of it?"

"Yep."

Wow. Maybe she hadn't given his position as foreman the respect it deserved. That was an enormous responsibility.

Brandon pulled her case and his duffle from the back of the truck. "Let's get you settled, then I'll show you around."

As they were climbing the steps to the porch, the front door opened and an elderly woman stepped out to greet them. She was tiny. Several inches shorter than Paige and petite to the point of looking frail. Her hair was short, pure white and curled in what her mom used to call a poodle perm. She wore purple tennis shoes, pink polyester pants and a boldly patterned Hawaiian shirt.

"Mr. Dilson," she said with a warm smile. "It's good to have you back."

"It's good to be back." He bent down to give her a squeeze and a kiss on the cheek, then he turned to Paige. "Ellie, this is Paige Adams. Paige, this is Ellie Williams. She's been the housekeeper at Copper Run Ranch since before I was born."

"So nice to meet you, Miss Adams," Ellie said, shaking her hand, and her firm grip said there was nothing frail about her. "Can I fix you two something to eat? We have stew leftover from supper."

"We picked up dinner before we left," Brandon said.

And he had refused to let Paige chip in half again. He always seemed intent on paying for everything, which she chocked up to male pride. And because of that she'd let him without argument. Besides, who was she to tell him how he should spend his money? It was actually kind of nice that someone *wanted* to do things for her for a change.

"Why don't I get you something to drink while you get your guest settled?" Ellie said.

"A beer would go down real well," Brandon said. "How about you, Paige? I'm sure Ellie could scrounge up a bottle of Chardonnay from the wine cellar."

His boss was kind enough to let them use the house. She didn't want to take advantage of his generosity by raiding the wine cellar, too. "Actually, water would be fine."

"Sure thing." Ellie pulled the door open. "You're in the guest room next to the master."

They stepped inside an enormous great room. The walls were built from richly stained wood and a wide stone fireplace rose up to kiss the peak of a vaulted, exposed beam ceiling. The decor was Southwestern-style with comfortable-looking furnishings in deep hues of primary colors, and thick, braided rugs covered the deeply polished wood floor. It was stylish, yet warm and welcoming. And spotless. As Brandon led her across the room to the staircase, she couldn't see as much as a speck of dust on any surface.

At the opposite end of the room was a set of double doors that Paige assumed led to the kitchen, because that's where Ellie headed.

"The house is amazing," Paige said as they reached the upstairs hallway that overlooked the great room below. "Your boss must be very wealthy."

"He does okay, I guess." He led her down the hall, pointing out the bathroom, then gesturing her inside one of the bedrooms. "Here it is."

It was large for a guest room, and decorated similarly as the main floor, only the furniture itself was a bit more rustic, and looked as though it could possibly be antique. The bed was only a full-size, but since they usually slept wrapped up in each other's arms, the lack of space wasn't a problem. On the nightstand sat a vase overflowing with flowers that Paige was guessing came from the beds out front.

Brandon set her case and his duffle on the bed. "This room doesn't have a private bath so we'll have to use the one in the hall."

"That's fine."

"You know," he said, taking her hand and pulling her to him, "we were in such a rush to leave, we didn't get any alone time today."

She grinned. "You're right, we didn't."

His arms slipped around her and he dipped his head to press a kiss to the side of her neck. She sighed and closed her eyes. "Maybe we should save that tour for tomorrow and turn in early, instead."

She slid her hands up his chest and looped them around his neck. "I am feeling awfully sleepy."

"Then I'm sorry to be the one to tell you, but I don't plan to let you get much sleep tonight."

She had suspected as much. And hoped. And prepared.

Since Brandon seemed to appreciate sexy lingerie, she went shopping during lunch and found a sexy, electric blue, lace bra and matching thong on the clearance rack at Victoria's Secret. She'd changed into them when she got home from work.

Brandon kissed his way up her throat, along her jaw, but just as his lips brushed hers, there was a soft knock at the door.

Paige looked up to see a man standing in the open doorway. He was big like Brandon and dressed like a cowboy in dusty jeans, boots and a brown cowboy hat, and a long-sleeved Western shirt.

"Hey, Bo—Brandon."

Brandon let go of her and said, "Paige, this is Clint Andersen, one of the men. Clint this is Paige Adams."

"Ma'am," Clint said, tipping his hat in greeting. He was kind of cute, in a rugged way. And he looked embarrassed to have caught them kissing. "I'm sorry to interrupt, but I was putting together the paperwork for tomorrow morning and I thought you should come down to the office and take a look at it before I print everything out. You know how I feel about computers. And the mares are ready if you want to take a look at them."

"I'll be right there."

He nodded. "Nice to have met you, ma'am," he told Paige, then disappeared down the hall.

"I guess that tour will have to wait, anyway," Brandon said.

"That's okay. Business first." It had to be a source of pride that he now had the skills to read the paperwork required for the job. And she was proud of him for all that he'd accomplished.

"This shouldn't take long," he said.

"No hurry. This will give me a chance to unpack."

He gave her a soft, lingering kiss, then headed out the door, closing it behind him. She heard the thump of his boots as he walked down the stairs.

She turned to the bed and unzipped her case. There was no

closet or chest of drawers, but there was a large pine armoire against the far wall. She pulled it open, the doors creaking on old hinges, and peeked inside. Empty hangers and a few spare blankets. She unpacked her clothes and hung them inside. Brandon's duffle sat there beside her case and she considered unpacking it for him, too, but she was afraid that would be too much like snooping. For all she knew he could have something private in there, not intended for her eyes. Which, of course, made her all the more curious. But after having had her belongings ransacked by her mom's boyfriends—not to mention money and jewelry taken—she appreciated the concept of privacy more than most. She wouldn't even go in Cheryl's desk for a pen without her express consent.

There was another rap at the door. Firmer this time. Then Ellie called out, "You decent?"

"Come in!"

The door opened and Ellie stepped inside. A bottle of water in one hand, a glass of wine in the other. "I thought I'd bring the wine, too, just in case you changed your mind."

She really didn't have to do that. "Are you sure it's okay?"

Ellie's brows rose. "You're not underage, are you?"

Paige laughed. "No, definitely not. It's just that it was very generous of your boss to let us stay in the house. I don't want to take advantage."

"I assure you, he won't mind a bit. He likes having guests in the house."

"Did Brandon ever have Ashleigh stay here?" Paige asked, realizing when she saw Ellie's frown, that it was none of her business *who* Brandon brought here. The question just sort of jumped out. Her cheeks burned with embarrassment. "I'm sorry, that was nosy of me. I don't even know why I asked. Forget I mentioned it."

"It's okay, I'm just surprised he told you about her. He doesn't talk about it much."

"He told me about her and the foreman."

"That woman broke his heart. For a while there I was worried he would never recover. This is the happiest I've seen him in a long time. And I'm sure that has a lot to do with you."

"I care about him a great deal," she said. More than she should, that was for sure.

"I can see that. But you should know, even though he doesn't let it show, and he sure wouldn't admit it, Brandon is still vulnerable. I don't want to see him hurt again."

Ellie clearly cared a great deal about him, too. But what she obviously didn't realize was that Brandon wasn't interested in a long-term relationship any more than Paige was. No one would be hurting anyone. She hoped.

The past few days, when she thought about not being close to Brandon, not seeing his sweet grin or feeling those big arms around her, there was an empty space inside her that made it hard to breathe.

But she would get over him. She didn't have a choice.

"I never had a boy of my own, but I've come to think of Brandon like a son."

"He's lucky to have you." When she lost her dad, none of the men her mother brought home had ever been able to replace him. Nor had they ever tried, or even wanted to. "And just so you know, hurting Brandon is the last thing I would ever want to do."

"Sometimes we hurt people whether we mean to or not."

Paige had learned that one the hard way. She was sure her mother hadn't intentionally hurt her, but still she had. And Ellie was obviously very protective of Brandon. But she must have seen something in Paige's eyes, heard something in her voice that made her believe what she said, because she smiled and said, "While Brandon finishes his business, why don't I give you a tour of the house?"

"I'd like that. And thank you for the flowers. Are they from the gardens out front?"

"Sure are," she said, pride beaming in her eyes. "It's always been a hobby for me. Although, I'm getting up in years, so it's harder for me to keep up. My knees are getting bad."

"They're so beautiful," Paige said. "Some of the flowers are in colors I've never seen before."

"I special order them." Ellie slipped an arm through hers. "Let's go have a look."

Paige wasn't sure why, but Ellie's acceptance was important to her. Which was a little silly since, after this weekend, chances were good that she would never see her again.

Brandon and Clint didn't finish up in the office, which was located in the main stable, until after nine-thirty.

"Sorry to take you away from your date," Clint said as Brandon shut down his computer.

He stacked the paperwork he'd just printed in his outbox and rose from his chair. "The ranch comes first. You know that."

"Well, it sure will be nice to have you back for good."

It hadn't been easy for Clint the past few months. He'd been with the ranch for over five years, yet he'd had no real experience as a foreman. But the night Brandon caught Mack, the former foreman, with Ashleigh, he'd told him to pack his things and get lost, and Clint seemed the logical replacement. Then, after only a few weeks on the job, Brandon had left for Vista del Mar and left Clint in charge. So not only had he taken on Mack's duties several days a week, but many of Brandon's several days a week, as well.

"I know I put a lot of pressure on you, and I want you to know that you've done one hell of a job."

"What Mack did to you…" He shook his head. "I'm not supposed to tell you this, but the night you fired him, a bunch of the guys followed him into town and taught him a lesson."

Brandon grimaced. A few of the men were rehabilitated ex-cons—a fact that would have given his father a coronary—who stood to lose a lot if they stepped even a hair outside of the law. But they were a loyal bunch of guys, and though Brandon didn't condone violence, he wasn't surprised they'd done it. "I'll pretend I didn't hear that."

"They only did it because they respect you. Besides, everyone sort of suspected something was going on between Ashleigh and Mack. We all felt pretty bad that no one told you."

"If it's any consolation, I wouldn't have believed you. She had me snowed."

"Paige, now she's a looker."

Brandon couldn't suppress a grin. "Yeah."

And the more he thought about it, the more he realized that he didn't want their relationship to end after the gala. The two-hour commute would be a bitch, especially with Paige's crazy work schedule, but he was sure they could work something out. Take turns traveling on alternate weekends maybe. Nothing too serious. Just a let's-see-how-things-go situation.

If she forgave him for lying to her, that is.

"I was surprised when you told me you were bringing her up," Clint said. "We talk at least every other day and you never mentioned you were even seeing someone."

"That's because I just met her last Friday."

His brows rose. "In the five and a half years I've worked here, including Ashleigh, you've brought home a grand total of three women. Paige must be pretty special."

"I've never met anyone quite like her."

"Then you might want to consider telling her who you really are. I'm no expert, but it seems like a relationship based on lies doesn't have a chance in hell of working out."

"I'll keep that in mind." Although technically, he hadn't lied that much. Not to her, personally. He just twisted the facts a little. "I better get back to the house."

"I know, butt out," Clint said. "You won't hear another word out of me about it. And by the way, the beard looks pretty good on you. You should think about keeping it when you come home."

"That's funny, because on my way out here Ellie said that

if I didn't shave it off the minute the truth was out, she would make the men hold me down and she would do it herself. And with a straight razor, so I would be sure to sit still."

Clint laughed because he knew Ellie would probably do it. "You go on in. I'll lock up."

Brandon grabbed his empty beer bottle and headed to the house. It was pitch-black out. He'd hoped to take Paige for a walk around the property, but it would have to wait until morning. At least with the paperwork for the sales mostly ready, and the horses prepared, he wouldn't have to be up at the crack of dawn. He also hoped the buyer was as serious as he'd led them to believe, and the purchase went quickly so he and Paige could set out early. He had a full day planned for them. And something very special planned for tonight, too. He stepped through the front door, wondering if Paige was still upstairs in the bedroom, when he heard voices from the kitchen.

He walked over and pressed his ear to the door and could hear Ellie and Paige talking. From the tone of the conversation, and the laughter, he would say the two of them were getting along well. Which would give him time to get everything ready.

Paige would never buy them having permission to sleep in his boss's bed, but there was nothing wrong with using his tub.

Twelve

Paige lost track of how long she and Ellie had been sitting there chatting, but when she'd polished off her third glass of wine, Brandon stuck his head in and asked, "Any chance I could steal my date back now?"

Ellie glanced at the clock over the industrial-size stove and said, "Good Lord, look at the time! I didn't realize how late it was."

"Well," Paige said, rising from her chair, "It was really nice talking to you. Thanks for the tour of the house. And keeping me company."

"Breakfast is at six sharp," Ellie said.

"You might want to keep something warm in the oven," Brandon said. Which she took to mean they would be up late, and wouldn't be awake that early. Then he took Paige's hand and pulled her along with him out of the kitchen and toward the stairs.

"Looks like you and Ellie hit if off," he said as they started up.

"We had a nice chat."

He glanced back at her warily. "Not about me I hope."

"Actually, no. We talked a lot about flowers, then I asked her what it was like living on a ranch and she was telling me stories. I figured it would be kind of…monotonous. But she makes it sound exciting."

"It can be. In good ways, and in bad ways, too. It's hard work."

Well, Paige definitely liked hard work. Although she was sure working on a ranch would be a lot more physical than sitting behind a desk planning parties. Not that she only did that. But she wasn't averse to physical labor—not that she was thinking of a career change.

Brandon led her down the hall, but when they got to the bedroom, he didn't stop. Instead, he took her to the master suite.

"What are we doing here?" she asked.

"It's a surprise."

She hesitated in the doorway. "But isn't this your boss's bedroom?"

"Yeah, but we're not using the bedroom." He tugged on her hand, and pulled her inside. The room was dark, so she couldn't see much more than the shapes of the furniture, but the smell of the room was weirdly familiar. Then she realized, it smelled like Brandon. He and his boss must wear the same aftershave. "Now, close your eyes," he said.

She wasn't sure why she should bother, since she could hardly see a thing anyway, but she closed them.

He stepped behind her, holding her upper arms to guide her as they walked into what she was assuming was the bathroom. "Okay, open them."

She opened her eyes and gasped at the scene before her. Dozens of lit candles around a whirlpool tub already filled with steaming water. On the ledge sat a bottle of champagne in ice and two flutes.

No, they definitely wouldn't be getting up at six.

"You like?" he asked.

"It's amazing." No one had ever taken the time to do something like this for her. She knew Brandon was a romantic, but she had never expected anything like this. But would his boss mind? "Are you sure this is okay?"

"Positive. In fact, my boss is the one who suggested it. And he left the champagne as a congratulations for my award." He turned her to him and began unbuttoning her shirt. When the sides parted, and he saw her new bra, he growled low in his throat.

"You like it?"

"I like it."

He cupped her breasts, grazed his thumbs across her nipples, watching as they hardened.

"There's more."

He didn't have to ask what she meant. A sexy grin curled his lips as he reached down to unfasten her jeans, then he eased them down her hips, revealing her barely there thong. "Nice."

"I went shopping at lunch."

He gazed at her, a hungry look in his eyes. "I really love seeing you in sexy underwear."

"And wearing it makes me feel sexy."

He looked down at his clothes. "Suddenly, I feel overdressed."

She slid her hands up his chest, tugging open the pearl snaps on his shirt. She pushed it down off his arms to the floor, sighing with pleasure at the way the candlelight danced across his skin. She unfastened his jeans and pushed them down.

"I hate to see these go," he said, turning her so he could unfasten her bra. "But the water is getting cold."

Her panties went next, then he flipped a switch beside the tub and the jets turned on. He got in first, then held her hand while she slipped in, pulling her into his lap, so she was straddling him. The water was just hot enough to be soothing, and the jets felt delicious on her skin. He reached for the champagne to pop the cork, and when she saw the label, she nearly swallowed her tongue.

"Brandon, that's *Cristal.*"

He shrugged. "So?"

"That's a *two-hundred-dollar* bottle of champagne."

The cork popped and some of the contents fizzed out. Brandon brought it to his lips and took a swig right from the bottle. Then he grinned and said, "Tastes like plain old champagne to me."

He poured two glasses and handed her one. She took a sip, letting it roll around on her tongue. It was…exquisite.

"I'll bet I know how it would taste even better," he said. He lifted his glass over her shoulder and she gasped as the icy liquid hit her. Brandon leaned forward and sucked it up, his mouth hot. He licked his lips and said, "I was right. Delicious."

"I can't believe you're wasting two-hundred-dollar champagne."

"I'm not wasting it. I'm enjoying it. You should try it."

Though it made her cringe to think of pouring anything so expensive literally down the drain, she poured a little bit over his collarbone, then quickly lapped it up. The fresh, fruity flavor mixed with the saltiness of his skin had an undeniable appeal.

He poured some of his on her opposite shoulder and licked it up with the flat of his tongue and the sensation made her shiver. Somehow she doubted this was what his boss had in mind when he left Brandon the bottle, but she couldn't imagine enjoying it more.

She did the same to him, then he poured lower, across her breast. The cold made her gasp in a breath, and as his hot mouth closed over the tip, sucked hard, she moaned and arched against him.

It went on like that until they had drained the entire bottle, finding new, creative ways to lick champagne from the other's body. If they hadn't been in the tub they would have been a sticky mess. And they were both so hot for each other by the time they made love that they got a little carried away, and sloshed water over the edge of the tub and onto the tile floor.

When the water in the tub cooled, they cleaned up the mess, wrapped themselves in big, fluffy towels and tiptoed back to the bedroom. Not that there was anyone up at eleven-thirty to hear them. According to Brandon, everyone rose before dawn, so Ellie went to bed early.

Paige wondered, since Brandon had to be up early, if they would go right to sleep when they got into bed, but he had other ideas.

They made love, then they talked for a while, mostly about the ranch and how it worked. They made love again, then snuck downstairs, her wrapped in a blanket, him in a sheet, and heated up some of that leftover stew, which they took upstairs and ate in bed. After two, with their stomachs full and their appetites for each other quenched, they curled up in each other's arms. Paige drifted off to sleep thinking how perfect the night had been, and how she wouldn't change a single thing. She also realized that she had more fun with Brandon just doing simple things, than she'd ever had with men she considered professionally successful and financially stable. Fancy dinners and nights at the theater were nothing compared to the closeness she and Brandon shared. If he never took her anywhere fancy, never bought her expensive jewelry or a big house, it couldn't change how she felt about him.

She loved him.

And it happened so…effortlessly. But their time was almost up. That meant she had exactly two weeks to fall out of love with him.

This was shaping up to be a really good day.

Good to his word, the breeder had purchased every mare

he'd expressed interest in, plus a young stallion that hadn't been part of their original deal. And he'd barely haggled on price. Brandon had to do a bit more paperwork, so the transaction had taken a little longer than expected, but now, with a check in his office and the horses loaded in the trailer, it was a done deal.

"That went better than I expected," Clint said as the trailer pulled away. "I thought he would try to get you to lower your price."

"I guess he knows a fair deal when he sees it. Or he just couldn't get a better deal from anyone else."

"I probably could have handled it on my own."

Brandon shrugged. "My ranch, my responsibility."

"You headin' out soon?"

"As soon as Paige is ready. Can you have Buttercup and Lucifer saddled up?"

"Sure thing Bo—I mean, *Brandon.*"

"You almost slipped up last night, too."

Clint flashed him a sheepish smile. "Sorry 'bout that. But I've called you boss for a long time. And you know that if I can't remember, the men won't, either. If I were you, I'd keep your lady friend away from the stables."

"I might just do that."

He left Clint and headed back to the house, wondering if Paige was up yet, and thinking of few fun ways he could wake her. He went in the kitchen door on the side, plucking a crimson tulip from the flower bed on his way past. Ellie was at the chopping block cutting up vegetables for soup, and the broth was boiling on the stove. "Paige up yet?"

"I heard her moving around up there, but she hasn't been down yet. Not an early riser, huh?"

"Usually she is," he said, then grinned. "But I didn't let her get much sleep."

She grimaced and shook her head. "I really didn't need to know that."

He laughed.

"What does she think of that horrid thing on your face?" she asked.

He stroked his beard. He'd always kept his face clean-shaven, and at first it had been a little uncomfortable, but he was actually getting used to it now. Even the longer hair was getting less annoying, but he was looking forward to going back to his normal, shorter cut. "She says she likes it."

"I hope that doesn't mean you're going to keep it. You have such a handsome face. You shouldn't keep it covered."

"I guess you'll just have to wait and see."

She shook her head, as if he was hopeless, and went back to slicing vegetables. "You're in a good mood. I guess the deal went well."

"Perfect."

"It's nice to see you happy for a change."

It was nice to feel happy. In fact, he'd been feeling that way a lot lately. "Did you see the list I left you?"

She gestured to the basket on the table. "I packed everything you asked for."

"You're a gem." He gave her a kiss on the cheek, and nabbed a carrot chunk from the cutting block. "I'm going to go fetch Paige."

He popped the carrot in his mouth on his way out of the kitchen and headed up the stairs to find Paige, realizing that, for the first time in a long time—a really long time—he felt great. Life was good.

Paige was in the bedroom, sitting on the bed. She had dressed in jeans and a long-sleeved, button-up shirt and was pulling on a pair of well-worn hiking boots. Her hair was pulled back in a ponytail. For a minute he leaned in the doorway, hiding the flower behind his back, and just watched her.

Damn, she was pretty. And while she looked good in a suit, with her hair fixed and her makeup flawlessly applied, he liked her better this way.

She looked up, saw him standing there watching her, and smiled. "Good morning. I didn't hear you come up."

"'Morning."

"Thanks for letting me sleep."

"Only seemed fair, since I kept you up so late."

She grinned and gestured to the window. "I saw them loading the horses. I take it business went well?"

"Without a hitch."

"Your boss will be happy, I'll bet."

"I'm sure he will."

"So," she said, glancing down at her outfit. "Am I dressed appropriately?"

He smiled. "Looks good to me. Although...I think something is missing."

She looked herself over. "A jacket?"

He pulled the flower from behind his back. "This."

She smiled, almost shyly, and took it. "It's beautiful. I'll put it in the vase, so it doesn't wilt."

She turned to do it and Brandon stepped up behind her, sliding his arms around her waist. "I had fun last night, by the way."

She sighed and closed her eyes, leaning back against him. "Me, too."

He pressed a kiss to the side of her neck, slipped a hand up under her shirt and laid it on her bare stomach.

She moaned softly and said, "If you don't stop that we'll never get out of here."

It was tempting to just undress her and spend the rest of the day in bed, but he had so much he wanted to show her.

He kissed her one last time then slipped his arms from around her. "Are you ready to learn to ride a horse?"

"I think so. I spent a few hours online the other night learning how."

Typical Paige. But she would find that reading about it and actually getting up in the saddle were very different.

They headed downstairs and Brandon grabbed the picnic basket on the way out. Buttercup and Lucifer were saddled up and ready to go. While he secured the basket to his saddle, Paige said, "I hope I'm riding the smaller horse."

"Sure are. Buttercup is old and gentle. She won't give you any trouble. Lucifer here doesn't like anyone but me riding him. He'll throw anyone else who gets on his back."

"What are all those lines across his skin?"

"Scars. He was severely abused. He's one of a few horses we took in from a rescue group a couple years ago. When he came to us he was skin and bones and terrified of all people." He rubbed Lucifer's neck. "I nursed him back to health, and since then I'm the only person he trusts. Isn't that right, boy?"

Lucifer whinnied and tossed his head, as if he understood what Brandon was saying.

"Why would someone hurt a defenseless animal?" Paige asked.

"There's no accounting for the things people do." He gave Lucifer one last pat and turned to Paige. "You ready?"

She nodded, looking a little nervous. "I think so."

He explained how to mount, then helped her up into the saddle and adjusted the stirrups. She looked wary at first, but he walked her around for several minutes to get a feel for it and she relaxed. When she looked comfortable he hoisted himself up on Lucifer's back. The horse was champing at the bit to run, but Brandon kept him at a slow pace as they started out, along the pasture and through the valley to the east pass. From there he took them up the rocky path, deeper into the mountains.

After half an hour or so he realized Paige was awfully quiet, so he looked back and asked, "You all right back there?"

She nodded enthusiastically. "I'm in awe. Everything is so beautiful, and the air is so clean. Your boss owns all of this?"

"This and a lot more."

"Where are we going, exactly?"

He shot her a grin. "You'll see."

"How long will it take to get there?"

"At this rate it should take another hour or so. Maybe a little longer."

They moved along in companionable silence, stopping occasionally to look at a plant that interested her, or to point out the wildlife. She gasped when two elk, a mother and baby, darted across the path in front of them several yards ahead.

"There isn't anything dangerous out here, is there?" she asked.

"Usually, if you leave the wildlife alone, it doesn't bother you."

"And if it does bother you?"

He patted the 12-gauge strapped to his saddle. "A warning shot typically does the trick."

Her eyes widened slightly. "I didn't even notice that."

"It's good to be prepared. But don't worry, you're safe with me."

Her smile said she trusted him. After all she went through as a kid, he knew that had to be hard for her.

They rode on, chatting about the terrain and the animals. There was so much he wanted to tell her, about coming up here during the summers and for school vacations. How he and Emma would go out exploring, even though his sister had always been more of a city girl.

Someday, he thought. Soon he would be able to tell her everything. Just a couple more weeks. The financial files were with the forensic accountant and he'd promised to have a report back to Brandon no later than the Wednesday before the gala. It was almost over.

The trail opened up into a grassy valley, bisected by Black Paw River.

He heard Paige gasp, and turned to see her gazing around in wonder.

"We're here," he said.

"It's gorgeous! And there's a waterfall!"

This used to be one of his favorite places as a kid. He couldn't count how many times he'd ridden up here when he was younger.

He dismounted near a patch of scrubby old pines then helped Paige down. She stretched and grimaced a little.

"Sore behind?"

"It is a little tender."

"You get used to it." He tied the horses to branches where they could graze, then unhitched the blanket and basket from his saddle while Paige walked to the riverbed.

"Can you swim in it?" she asked, as he spread the blanket out several feet from the water.

"Only if you want to freeze your tail off. That water is cold. But there's a hot spring about a quarter mile up from here. We'd have to walk to it, though."

"I didn't bring a bathing suit."

He wouldn't have let her wear it if she had.

"So, what now?" she asked, sitting on the blanket.

He settled in beside her. "Whatever you want."

Today they had no schedule, no agenda, no pressing deadlines to worry about. Today was all about doing whatever they wanted, even if that meant doing nothing at all.

Thirteen

Paige laid back on the blanket, the sun on her face, her belly full with the thick roast beef sandwiches and creamy potato salad they had eaten for lunch, listening to the gentle rush of the river at her side. So far, this had been a perfect day. She could see why Brandon loved it here, why he would never leave. She wouldn't, either.

She tried to imagine what it would be like if Brandon didn't just work the ranch, but owned it. If they were married and she lived here. As much as she loved her career, would she give it up for this?

It was a silly notion. Because not only did Brandon not own it, he would never ask her to come live here with him. He didn't want a commitment.

But what if he did? What if he changed his mind and he asked her to move here? Would she consider leaving everything to be with him? The realization that her answer wasn't an immediate "absolutely not," was a bit shocking.

It would mean giving up her security and relying on someone

other than herself to take care of her. She couldn't imagine ever doing that. Not with someone in a career as unstable as Brandon's. She'd been doing research on the internet about ranching, and foremen's duties and what they made per year. If Brandon's boss paid him the average for this region, including room and board, he wouldn't be making much. Though she hated that it mattered to her, it did.

"Hey, you falling asleep on me?" Brandon asked from beside her.

She opened her eyes. He was on his stomach, propped up on his elbows. She shook her head. "Just thinking."

"About what?"

"How this has been the perfect day."

"It's not over yet." He rolled onto his side, scooting close.

She reached up and cupped the side of his face, felt the familiar softness of his beard against her palm, and couldn't help wondering what he would look like without it. "Right now, I feel too relaxed to move."

"That's okay," he said, toying with the top button on her shirt. "All you have to do is lie there while I make you feel good."

"Here?"

"Why not?" He popped open the top button, then the next. "We're all alone."

"There's no chance anyone will come up here?"

He shook his head. "No reason to."

Well, if he was sure…

He unfastened the rest of the buttons and eased the sides apart, then he lowered his head and pressed a kiss to the swell of her breast, just above the cup of her bra. It felt so good, she decided to take him at his word.

"And if it makes you more comfortable," he said, reaching down to unfasten her jeans, slipping his hand inside, "We can leave most of our clothes on."

In theory it was a great idea, right up until the minute she realized that she wouldn't be satisfied until he was inside her, and that just wasn't going to be possible with their clothes on. And by then, as they undressed each other, she was too turned on to care who might be around. A week with the man and suddenly she was a budding exhibitionist.

After they made love they covered up with the blanket and cuddled for a bit, but it started to get too warm in the sun. Brandon suggested they head back to the ranch, freshen up, then go into Wild Ridge for dinner.

Though her behind was a little sore, the ride back was actually easier. When they reached the valley and the ranch came into view, Lucifer stomped the ground and tossed his head, which would have scared the hell out of her if she were the one on his back.

"He wants to run," Brandon explained, pulling back on the reins. "He gets restless."

"You can go if you want."

"You sure? Buttercup will take you right back to the stable."

"Sure, go ahead."

He turned Lucifer in the opposite direction of the ranch, barely tapped his boot heels against the horse's sides and made a clicking noise, and Lucifer shot off like a rocket.

Paige watched in awe as they bolted across the grassy expanse, so in tune with one another it was hard to tell where the animal ended and he began. Clearly, Brandon was born to ride a horse.

Though it would never make him financially successful, there was no doubt he belonged here on the ranch. It was in his blood.

When he was too far to see clearly she tapped the horse's belly with her heels, the way Brandon taught her, and Buttercup ambled back in the direction of the ranch. Paige was by no stretch of the imagination a natural on a horse, but she had enjoyed the ride and was beginning to feel more confident. She was a little sad that she would probably never ride one again.

She'd just made it to the stable when Brandon galloped up beside her, a little windblown, but looking happy. He dismounted, then helped her down.

"Go on in the house and get cleaned up. I'm going to give Lucifer a quick rubdown. I'll be up in a bit."

Paige was a little sweaty from the ride back, so she decided to take a quick shower, then Brandon came in the bathroom and got in with her, and gave *her* a rubdown, too.

When they were dressed, they climbed into the truck and drove to Wild Ridge. Brandon explained that it used to be a mining town in the 1800s, and was now a thriving tourist spot. Paige could see, as they pulled down the main strip, that it had retained its old-West charm. The town was rustic, but well-maintained with a slew of shops and attractions to appeal to the tourists.

Brandon took her to a brewery where the hostess knew him by name, and though there were other people waiting, she seated Brandon and Paige immediately. The benefits of being a local, she assumed. They drank beer, ate burgers and Brandon even managed to coax her out onto the dance floor a few times.

It seemed as though every time she thought she and Brandon couldn't have more fun, he somehow managed to show her an even better time. Or maybe it was just that being with him made her very happy. She'd never known anyone like him. Though she hated the overused term, for lack of a better description, he was "real." What you saw was what you got. No illusions, no pretenses. Just a sweet, charming, *good* man.

She had planned to nab the check so Brandon wouldn't have to pay again, but as usual he beat her to it. When she put up a fuss he said, "My turf, my responsibility."

There was always some excuse why he should be the one to pay. But one of these days she would take *him* out.

They didn't get back to the ranch until after midnight. She was just a little tipsy from the beer, and must have been exhausted from the busy day. She crawled into bed to wait for Brandon while he used the bathroom, and when she opened her eyes again, it was morning.

"Good morning, sleepyhead."

She sat up and rubbed her eyes. Brandon was standing by the armoire getting dressed. His hair was wet and a damp towel hung over the footboard. "What time is it?"

"A little after eight-thirty. You sure went out like a light last night. I left the room for two minutes and when I came back you were out cold."

She yawned and stretched. "You should have woken me."

He shrugged and pulled a T-shirt over his head. "I think we both needed a good night's rest."

"But it was my last night here."

He walked around the bed and sat on the edge of the mattress beside her. "Maybe it doesn't have to be."

She wished that were possible. "You know I need to get back and work."

"I don't mean now." He reached up to touch her cheek, tucked her hair behind her ear. "Maybe you could come back after the gala."

Her breath caught. "You would want me to? I mean, I thought we agreed that after the gala we would be done."

"Is that what you want?"

No. Not at all. And though part of her wanted to jump at the opportunity to keep seeing him, she knew from experience that long-distance relationships had a way of not working out. Besides, she and Brandon had no future. Their lives were too different.

But was she really ready to make that decision? Couldn't they just take more of a wait-and-see stance?

"Let's not make any definite plans," she said. "Let's just… see how things go."

He shrugged. "Fair enough."

She would have expected him to be at least a little disappointed. Instead, it seemed as though it didn't really matter either way to him. Maybe he had only asked because he thought it was what she wanted, and he could take her or leave her.

He grabbed his socks from the foot of the bed. He pulled them on, followed by his boots. Then he looked at her and his brow lowered. "Hey, you okay?"

She must have looked as conflicted as she felt. She forced a smile and nodded. "Still half-asleep, I guess."

"Well, get up. We have to get on the road." He gave her a quick, minty kiss then rose to his feet. "We've been so busy, I haven't had the chance to show you around the stables. You want to take a quick tour before we head out?"

"I'd like that."

"Why don't you get ready to go, then meet me outside?"

"I won't be long."

He left and she climbed out of bed. She cleaned up and got dressed, then packed her things back into her case. She wished she could stay longer, but it was probably better that she didn't. It could be too easy to get caught up in the fantasy. She had to get back to her real life, to what was really important. She carried her bag down to the great room and set it by the door, then went to the kitchen so she could say goodbye to Ellie and thank her for her hospitality, but she wasn't around.

She headed outside. Yesterday when they left for their ride, the stables had been bustling with activity. Maybe it was because it was early, or a Sunday, but no one was around. She found Brandon in the larger stable, in what she assumed was the business office. He sat at the desk, in front of the computer, staring intently at whatever was on the screen while typing at an impressive pace for someone who had just learned how to read.

"You're fast," she said.

Brandon jolted at the sound of her voice. "You startled me. I didn't hear you come in."

He hit a few more keys, clicked the mouse, then switched the monitor off.

"How did you learn to type like that?"

He rose from the chair. "A computer program at the library. I practice in my free time."

He seemed nervous. Flustered. Maybe it was better that she didn't mention his reading skills, since it obviously made him uncomfortable.

"Have you seen Ellie?" she asked. "I wanted to say good-bye."

"Church. Along with most of the men. She makes them go. She says it keeps them honest."

She wondered if that meant that Brandon usually went, too. For some reason, that was hard to picture. "I guess that's why it's so quiet around here."

"Sundays are like that. You ready for that tour?"

She nodded. "Ready."

Taking her hand, he walked her through the larger stable first, then the smaller one. She had assumed the smell of the fresh hay mixed with the pungent aroma of the animals would have been unpleasant, and was surprised to find that she sort of liked it. And the animals themselves were beautiful. Some were so huge they towered over her, while others were smaller breeds. She didn't know what most of the equipment was for that he pointed out, and the terminology was unfamiliar to her, but Brandon clearly knew his stuff. The more she saw of the operation, of him in action, the more impressed she was.

After they had taken a quick walk through the barn, Paige noticed the long, narrow building set farther to the back.

"Is that where the men sleep?"

"Yep."

"Can I see it?"

He shrugged. "Sure. I doubt anyone is there right now, anyway."

If Paige needed a reality check, something to kill the fantasy, seeing the ranch hands' quarters did the trick. The building was comprised of a kitchen area with two tables long enough to hold at least a dozen men each, and a social area with couches and chairs and an older-looking, large-screen television with a big, rabbit-eared antenna on top. A second, larger room was the communal sleeping area. Rows of bunk beds lined the walls on either side, all neatly made. There were doors on the opposite end, which she assumed led to the bathrooms.

It looked disturbingly similar to the women's shelter she and her mom had stayed in when they lost their trailer, and just standing in the doorway set her nerves on edge, brought her back to that time.

She couldn't imagine ever living that way again. The possibility scared the hell out of her. "You said the foreman gets his own place?"

"It's around back. I'd show it to you, but Clint is using it. It's a lot like your apartment, but all one room. And about half the size."

Meaning the entire residence couldn't have been much larger than her living room. For a single guy that probably wasn't too bad, but what if the foreman decided to get married?

It didn't matter either way to her, because despite how she felt about Brandon, seeing this part of his life was a stark reminder of why their relationship would never be more than an affair. They were just too different.

And how many times would she have to tell herself that before it finally started to sink in?

Her anxiety must have shown, because Brandon put a hand on her shoulder and gave it a gentle squeeze. "You okay?"

She manufactured a smile. "Fine. Just a little tired, I guess."

"Well, why don't we get going. You can sleep on the way if you want."

"I may just do that."

They gathered their things and loaded up the truck and were on the road before ten. Paige leaned her seat back and closed her eyes, but she couldn't sleep. She didn't want to talk, either, so she sat motionless, so he would think she was dozing, and listened to him sing along with the radio. Didn't it just figure that he had an above-average singing voice? The man was perfect in every way. Well, every way except the one that really mattered to her.

And the irony of the situation was that even if she could change him, she wouldn't want to. She was the one with the problem, the issues. *She* was flawed, not him. He was fine just the way he was, and she didn't deserve him. And it was clear that the longer she let this drag on, the harder it would be to pull away later.

Though this past week had been one of the happiest in her life, it was time to let go.

Fourteen

Since Brandon dropped her off at her apartment Sunday, Paige had been an emotional wreck. All she had to do was think about Brandon and her eyes started to well. And she *never* cried. She'd broken up with guys she'd been seeing for months and hadn't felt nearly this awful. And she hadn't even broken up with him yet!

She'd spent most of the ride home preparing herself, but as he'd carried her bag to her door and said goodbye, she hadn't had the guts to say the words.

She spent the next three days trying to work up the courage to do it, avoiding his calls for fear that hearing his voice would crack the hard shell she was trying desperately to erect around her heart.

She finally went to his hotel room Wednesday night to talk, to tell him it was over, but he opened the door and she saw him standing there looking so adorable and so happy to see her. The next thing she knew she was in his arms kissing him, tears streaming down her face.

She could see Brandon was confused by her emotional meltdown, but he didn't question it. He just kissed her tears away, then made love to her so sweetly, so passionately, she knew it was hopeless. She couldn't end it. Not yet.

That was five days ago, and she had seen him practically every night since. And now they only had five days until the gala, when they would end things for good. Yet, every time she thought about their relationship being over, she got a knot in her chest so tight she could barely breathe. Somehow she was the happiest, and most miserable, she'd ever been in her life.

Poor Cheryl didn't know what to think of Paige's sudden change in personality. They'd worked together for almost three years and Paige had never been so fragile. It made her think of her mom, and the way she used to act after Paige's dad died. The idea that she was anything like her mom scared the hell out of her. And brought her to tears for about the tenth time that day.

"Margaret Cole just faxed over the final seating chart for the wedding Friday," Cheryl said, stepping into her office and handing her the sheet, then she saw Paige swipe at the tears hovering precariously on her lower lids. "Oh, sweetie, not again."

"I don't know what's wrong with me," Paige said, grabbing a tissue and dabbing at her drippy nose. "You know me. I don't do this. I don't *cry.* I don't even find Hallmark commercials particularly moving. And look at me. I'm an emotional train wreck."

"Maybe you have a hormone imbalance. Or maybe it's just really bad PMS."

That was possible. Although she didn't usually get weepy. Just a little edgy. But all the added stress could be making it worse. And if that was it, as soon as her period started she should be feeling back to her old self again. "Maybe that's it," she told Cheryl, feeling hopeful for the first time in a week.

"When is your period due?"

"Soon, I think." She'd been so busy lately she hadn't given it much thought. She opened the calendar on her computer and counted the days, then, positive she'd made a mistake, she counted them again. As she counted them a third time, just to be sure, her heart bottomed out. "Oh, damn."

Cheryl frowned. "What's wrong?"

"My last period was thirty-one days ago."

"Is that a long time for you?"

"Since I was twelve I've started every twenty-eight days like clockwork." She looked up at her friend, heart in her throat. "Cheryl, my period is late."

Damned broken condom, Paige thought as she waited for Cheryl to get back from the pharmacy with the home pregnancy test.

She closed her eyes and breathed deep, struggling to stay calm. How had she let this happen? This wasn't part of the plan. She'd always imagined she'd have kids someday, but only after she found the right man. And only after her business was established. This just wasn't a good time.

And what about Brandon? What would he think of this? Considering his financial situation, and his current living arrangements, she doubted he would be thrilled with the idea of starting a family. Especially with a woman he never intended to have a lasting relationship with.

Maybe learning that she didn't expect a thing from him, that financially she could care of the baby herself, would take some of the pressure off. It might be rough for a year or two, but she would tighten the belt and squeeze by. And with any hope, the gala would go off without a hitch, bringing her a few high-profile clients, which would generate the resources to hire a few extra employees. Because, while Cheryl was worth her weight in gold, she already performed far above what was expected of her. Like going out and fetching her boss pregnancy tests in the middle of a workday.

But first she had to find out for sure if she really was pregnant. There was still a slight possibility it was something else. Some kind of weird, stress-induced chemical imbalance. One not caused by a fetus.

She heard the outer door open and Cheryl called, "I'm back!"

Paige's heart began to race. Cheryl appeared in her office doorway, red-faced and out of breath, with a small white bag.

"You ready for this?" she asked.

God, no. But putting it off wasn't an option.

Though Paige prided herself on being calm and rational in every situation, her hands were trembling as she took the bag, and as she walked across the hall to the restroom and locked herself inside, her knees felt squishy.

She opened the box, pulled out the test wand, and, since she had never actually used one before, skimmed the directions. It only took a few seconds to take the test, then she waited, staring at the indicator window, willing it with her mind to be negative.

It was supposed to take three to five minutes to marinate, but after about thirty seconds the result, which would say either *pregnant* or *not pregnant* began to appear.

Pregnant.

"Crap."

She sat there for a couple of minutes more, on the verge of hyperventilation, hoping the word *not* would suddenly materialize and everything would be okay.

She heard a soft knock on the door. "You okay in there, honey?"

Nope. Not at all. She pulled the door open and held it up so Cheryl could see the results.

Cheryl sucked in a soft breath. "Oh, boy."

"Yeah."

What was she going to tell Brandon?

She could simply *not* tell him. Odds were, after the gala she would never see him again. He would never even know about the baby. Wouldn't it just be easier on him that way?

But could she deny her child the privilege of knowing its father? Even if its father wasn't exactly thrilled about it? Or maybe she wasn't being fair, maybe Brandon would be excited to learn he was going to be a dad. He was a stand-up kind of guy. He might even want them to be a family.

She cringed at the thought of the three of them packed into the tiny foreman's quarters. And where would she work? What would she do for a living up there? Unless she had a decent paying job they could never afford anything bigger. She didn't even know if he was *allowed* to live off the ranch, or if the job required him to stay on the property. And if he lost his job, what then? Where would they go? What would they do for money?

The panicked feeling was back, clawing at her insides.

No, moving to the ranch with Brandon was definitely out of the question.

"So," Cheryl said, "What are you going to do?"

The only thing she could do at this point. "I guess I'm going to have a baby."

Something was up with Paige.

She hadn't been the same since they got back from the ranch. Brandon had dropped her at home, then they hadn't talked again for several days. He'd tried phoning her cell a few times Monday and Tuesday, but it always went to voice mail and she didn't return his calls. Concerned, he drove into town a day early, leaving a message with her secretary to call him. She'd shown up at his motel Wednesday night unannounced and practically threw herself in his arms. Then she started crying, which had really baffled him. But when he asked her later what was wrong, she said the stress from work was getting to her, and she would be better after the gala was over. He didn't push the issue, but he had the distinct feeling it was more than that. He even decided to stay in town until the gala. If she was that stressed out, he figured she could use the moral support. And maybe he just wanted to be close to her. But he'd seen her nearly every night since then and she'd seemed okay. And the sex had been beyond fantastic.

The truth is, he was looking forward to the gala being over, as well. Hiding the truth from her was starting to get to him. Only five more days and Paige would know the truth. Up until now he'd been pretty confident she would be willing to forgive his twisting of the facts—and a few outright lies—but he was starting to get a little nervous.

Whether Paige wanted to admit it or not, they were good together. After her visit to the ranch he'd pretty much made the decision that he wanted her in his life permanently. He'd been with Ashleigh two years before he was ready to move her into his home, but with Paige, he wouldn't hesitate to clear one side of the closet for her right now. Which was so *not* like him, he couldn't help trusting it. Which he knew made no sense at all.

There was a knock at his motel room door and Brandon looked at his watch. It was barely four. Way too early for Paige. She didn't usually leave work until after seven. He snapped his laptop shut and slid it under the bed. He walked to the door and checked out the window, surprised to see Paige standing there, still in her work clothes. He took a quick glance around the room for incriminating evidence, then opened the door. The minute he saw her face he knew something was wrong.

She was white as a sheet.

"What's the matter?" he said.

She sighed. "I look that bad, huh?"

He gestured her inside, then shut the door behind her. She walked over to the bed and sat on the edge of the mattress. "We need to talk."

"Okay." He pulled out one of the chairs at the table and sat. "Let's talk."

"There's really no good way to say this, no way to soften the blow, so I'm just going to say it. I'm pregnant."

Whoa. That was truly the last thing he'd expected her to say. And for several seconds, words escaped him. She sat there looking anxious, waiting for him to say something, and though usually he had an opinion about pretty much everything, he was at a loss.

She was pregnant. With his baby. He was going to be a dad.

"You're angry," she said, cringing, as though she were expecting him to suddenly erupt.

"Surprised, yes, but not angry." Why would he be? It wasn't anyone's fault. In fact, when he peeled back the top layers, to the emotions lurking under the surface, he was a little stunned to discover that he was sort of...happy. Excited even, in a shell-shocked way.

A baby with Paige. Why not?

"You're sure?" he asked.

"I took a home pregnancy test. I understand they're pretty reliable. Plus my period is late, and it's never late. And I don't know if you noticed, but I've been a little...emotional lately."

Yeah, he'd noticed, and if he knew Paige better, he probably would have figured out why. "So, you're sure."

She nodded. "Yeah, I'm sure."

He took a deep breath and blew it out. "Wow."

"So," she said, looking nervous, like she was waiting for the other shoe to drop. "What do you think we should do?"

Good question. And the answer came to him faster than he would have imagined. It was what he wanted. "I think you should marry me."

Apparently the last thing she had been expecting was a marriage proposal, because her jaw literally dropped. "Marry you?"

"And move out to the ranch. We both know what broken homes are like. We can't do that to our child."

"But—"

"I know it's soon, but I think we owe it to the baby to be a family. To at least try."

"Where will I work? I doubt the people of Wild Ridge are champing at the bit for an image consultant-slash-event planner. How will I make a living?"

"You won't have to. I'll take care of you. You and the baby." He needed to tell her the truth, the consequences be damned. He couldn't lie to her any longer. Not now. "Paige, there's something I should tell you—"

"Brandon, I can't. I have a career, a life here. I've worked my tail off to make my company a success. I can't just give that up."

"This is no longer about what we want. It's about what's best for the baby. Besides, I can give you everything you need."

"Financial security? Can you give me *that?*"

Something dark and cold settled over him. "Are you suggesting that I don't make enough money?"

"It's more complicated than that. How will you fit a wife and a baby in the foreman's quarters? And without me working, how could we ever afford better?"

"Better? So what I am right now isn't good enough for you?"

"That isn't what I meant. You know what it was like for me when I was a kid. I just can't go through that again, or put my own child though it."

Wow, that was brutal. "Now you think I'll be a lousy father, too?"

"No! I didn't say that. But I've worked damned hard to be self-sufficient. You can't expect me to give that up."

"So, if I were to leave the ranch and get a job as an executive, pushing paper in some office, bringing home a salary with benefits, and I asked you to marry me, you would say yes?"

"Brandon—"

"Would you say yes?"

"I would *never* ask you to leave the ranch. You *belong* there. It's what makes you happy."

"But that's not good enough for you, is it?" So much for Paige being different. She didn't think he was good enough. She'd just been slumming it.

He should have known. And the truth stung more than he could have imagined. He'd let himself care again, let himself trust, and once again he'd been burned.

If she had said yes, if she had married him, would he have come home one day to find her in the stable with one of his men?

"You know, you're absolutely right. Marrying someone like you would have been a monumental mistake."

"Brandon—"

"Forget it. I don't know what I was thinking. Why would I want to marry a woman I don't even love?"

She flinched, and though it should have given him satisfaction to know he'd hurt her, he only felt like a piece of garbage, regurgitating back the words Ashleigh had spat at him the day she left.

"Just so you know, I won't hold you financially responsible for the baby. I'm prepared to raise this child entirely on my own, if necessary."

He felt as if she'd punched him in the stomach. "Do you honestly expect me to just give up my rights? To move on with my life and forget I'm responsible for bringing a child into this world? You're even more selfish and narcissistic than I could have imagined."

Her eyes widened and she shook her head. "I didn't mean—"

"Let's get one thing straight, sweetheart. This is my baby, too, and I'll be damned if I'm going to let you shut me out of its life just because you think I'm not good enough. For the next eighteen years and nine months, you're *stuck* with me."

"Of course." Tears welled in her eyes and she lowered them to her lap, wringing her hands. "I never meant to hurt you."

"Didn't you know, you can't hurt someone who doesn't give a damn. You mean nothing to me." He only wished that were true. He felt betrayed. Rubbed raw, all the way to his soul.

"Maybe we should talk about this later, when we've both had time to think about things."

As far as he was concerned, there was nothing left to say. He got up and opened the door.

As she walked past him, tears rolling down her cheeks, he had to stop himself from grabbing her and pulling her into his arms.

She was no better than Ashleigh, and all of the women who had come before her. And to think that he'd almost told her the truth. Had she known about his millions two seconds sooner he doubted she would have been so quick to refuse his proposal. And then he would be stuck with her. Another woman who only wanted him for his money.

Thank God he'd kept his mouth shut.

He packed his things, checked out of his room, and drove back to Copper Run. Where he belonged.

The Tanner/Cole wedding was going off without a hitch. Dinner had been served, the bride and groom had cut the cake and had their first dance, and it would be another half hour before it was time to throw the bouquet. Excellent timing, since the intermittent nausea Paige had been experiencing for the last few days was suddenly back.

Since greasy foods only exacerbated the problem, she should have known better than to scarf down half a dozen bacon-wrapped scallops. But they had tasted so yummy, it seemed like a good idea at the time. Not to mention that she hadn't been eating enough lately. Every time she thought of a certain person, she felt utterly sick inside.

But she wasn't allowed to think about that now. Not until the job was completed. Which meant in precisely one hour she could get in her car, drive the ten minutes home, and fall apart. Which had been the routine every night this week.

She knew she had hurt Brandon, wounded his pride, and they really needed to talk about what they planned to do. She'd gone back to the motel the day after their fight but he had already checked out. She'd tried his cell phone several times but it always went to voice mail. She never left a message, for fear that she would dissolve into tears halfway through and look completely pathetic. She'd considered driving up to Copper Run to talk to him, to try to explain her side of things, and tell him how sorry she was, but the possibility that he would only reject her again kept her from making the trip. Still, she missed him terribly. The loneliness, the sense of loss, was absolute, like a living, breathing thing, feeding off her anguish. And there was a pain in her heart, an acute ache that wouldn't go away.

The idea that she refused his proposal over something so trivial as money gnawed at her. What did it matter how much money he made, or where he lived? The only thing that mattered was that they were together. A family. So maybe things would have been tight for a while. So what? She'd been through tough times before. She could handle it. At least they would be together. And with the thriving tourist trade in Wild Ridge, there was bound to be someone who could use the expertise of an event planner. Maybe she could even relocate her business. She would never make as much money as she could being closer to a big city, but making lots of money had never been the point. The point had been to feel secure. To be… happy. And when she was with Brandon, she was. Happier than she'd ever been in her life.

Maybe it was foolish, and irresponsible—everything she'd worked so hard not to be—but if she could go back in time to the minute when he asked her to marry him, she would tell him yes, without hesitation. It was just that he'd surprised her with his proposal and she hadn't had time to think it through.

She never made any decisions without considering all aspects of the situation. It was just who she was.

None of that made a difference now. Like he said, he didn't love her. He only wanted to marry her for the baby's sake. That didn't make her feel any less empty inside, love him any less.

Tears welled in her eyes and she blinked them away. *This* was why she wasn't allowed to think of him until after work.

"Miss Adams?"

Paige turned to find a very pregnant Emma Larson standing behind her. In her hand she held a small plate of those unholy little bacon-wrapped scallops, and as the smell wafted her way, Paige's stomach heaved.

No barfing in front of the wedding guests.

She swallowed hard and pasted on a smile. "Hello, Ms. Larson. It's so nice to see you again."

"I just wanted to tell you what a lovely reception this has been. If the gala tomorrow night is half as beautiful we're in for a treat."

She tried to look anywhere but Emma's plate. "That's very kind of you to say."

"The next time I plan a party you'll be the first person I call. And you'll have to give me the number of the caterer you used. Dinner was fantastic."

"I'm sure I have their card in my planner," Paige said, unable to look away as Emma took a nibble of a scallop. It looked both delicious and horrendous at the same time.

"I really shouldn't be eating these," she said, "but lately I'm so starving I eat everything that isn't tied down." She popped the last bite in her mouth and bile rose in Paige's throat.

Oh, boy.

"Excuse me, please," she said, slapping a hand over her mouth and darting for the ladies room. Thank goodness it was close, because Paige barely made it into a stall before she lost the appetizers, and what little else she had eaten that day. It was quick, violent and physically draining.

Oh, this was fun.

When she was finished she wiped her mouth with tissue, flushed the toilet and dragged herself to her feet. She opened the stall, horrified to find standing there not only several wedding guests, but the bride, Margaret Tanner. Emma had apparently followed her inside. Gillian Preston, who worked for the *Seaside Gazette* was also there, along with Ana Rodriguez.

How utterly embarrassing.

"You okay?" Margaret asked Paige as she crossed to the sink to rinse her mouth. "Tell me it's not food poisoning."

"I'm okay. And no, it's not food poisoning. Your guests are safe." Unless pregnancy had become a contagious condition, that is. But barfing must have done the trick, because she no longer felt nauseous. Just a little weak, and she was sure that would pass. If she was more careful with what she ate in the future, maybe she could avoid a repeat performance.

"It will get better," Emma said. "I was sick through my third month, then it just went away. I've felt fantastic ever since."

"When I was pregnant with my son the first few months were pretty rough," Gillian piped in. "It does get easier."

"Unless you have the flu," Ana said, shooting a look to Emma. "In which case you should feel better in a day or two."

Paige could tell the women were hoping for an explanation, and she saw no reason not to tell them the truth. It wasn't like it was a big secret. "It's not the flu."

"Well then, congratulations!" Emma said, and Gillian asked, "How far along are you?"

"Not very. I only just found out Monday, and with the gala tomorrow, I haven't had time to see my doctor yet." But she had found a pregnancy calendar online and it said the baby was due January twenty-second. Which was an eerie, cosmic sort of coincidence considering both she and Brandon were born on the same day. That had to be some kind of sign. Didn't it?

But she didn't believe in signs. Isn't that what she'd told Brandon?

"You and the father must be so excited," Margaret said.

"Actually, this was a little unexpected. The father...he's not..." She was mortified to feel tears well in her eyes again. She forced a laugh, but it emerged sounding strangled and pathetic. "It's complicated."

Emma touched her arm. "Welcome to the club, sweetie. Everyone here pretty much went through hell, but look at us now, all happy."

"Look at Will and me," Margaret said. "We started out pretending to be engaged, never guessing for a second that we would actually fall in love. But here we are, married for real and amazingly happy."

"And I spent months trying to take down Max's boss," Gillian said. "And he more or less blackmailed me into marrying him. I guess when you love someone, it's easy to overlook the bad stuff."

Emma gave Paige's arm a squeeze. "It'll work out. I promise."

"Well, I should get back to my groom, before he thinks I fell in," Margaret joked, fluffing her hair.

"And I have to check in with the babysitter," Gillian said, digging in her purse for her cell phone. "Ethan had a case of the sniffles earlier today."

"And I should find Ward before some pretty young thing tries to swoop down and steal him from me," Ana joked, but her smile said she was anything but worried. "For what it's worth, we had a pretty rocky start, and we couldn't be happier now. Although it's always an adventure being with a rock star."

"I'm sure everything will work out," Paige said. The problem was, she *wasn't* sure. She prided herself on keeping her life in order, but since Brandon came along, everything was all mixed up. For the first time, she didn't have her next moved plotted out. She was flying blind.

Emma slipped her arm through Paige's. "Why don't we go find a quiet corner and chat?"

Paige looked at her watch. "I really need to get things ready for the bouquet toss."

"I think the bouquet can wait."

She nodded and they walked—well, Emma waddled—to the back corner where there were empty tables. Margaret and William were chatting with their guests and she spotted Gillian and Max dancing. Ward was signing autographs on paper napkins for a group of giggly young girls while Ana looked on with nothing but love and pride. They did all look happy.

Paige barely knew Emma, and she didn't make it a habit of pouring her heart out to a virtual stranger, but it felt good to get it off her chest. And learning that Emma had been in a similar situation—an accidental pregnancy with a man she had just met—gave her hope that everything would be okay. Even if they could never be together, she at least needed to be sure he knew how much she respected him, and what a good father she knew he would be.

There wouldn't be time before the gala, but when it was over she and Brandon were going to talk. Whether he wanted to hear her out or not.

Brandon had spent the rest of the week at the ranch. He tended to the horses, chopped wood, ran to town for supplies, anything to keep his mind off what had started as a nagging suspicion, and had now festered into an undeniable fact.

He was a jerk.

Saturday afternoon, when he should have been getting ready to leave for the gala, he sat in the grass at the foot of his mother's grave, in the family plot about a quarter mile from the house, repulsed by the realization that he had been so jaded by the women in his life, so used to being disappointed, that he'd come to expect it. He had condemned Paige without even bothering to try to see things from her point of view. Without letting her explain. Not that she needed to.

He may have had his share of problems growing up, but he'd never once had to worry if he would lose the roof over his head, or where his next meal was coming from. He'd never set foot in a homeless shelter, much less had to live in one. He had no idea what it was like to *not* have money. So naturally he had just assumed that when she said she needed security, that was code for material excess. Big houses and fancy cars. When deep down, in his heart, he knew that Paige was one of the least materialistic women he'd ever met.

Knowing what she'd gone through, and how hard she had worked to overcome her past, he'd had the gall to expect her to just give it all up, to take it on faith that an uneducated ranch hand, a man she had known for less than three weeks, was going to take care of her.

And really, what reason had he given her that would make her want to marry him? To give up everything that was important to her?

It's what's best for the baby. Jesus. How romantic was that? He hadn't even had the decency to get down on one knee. To tell her he loved her. In retrospect, if she *had* said yes, he might be seriously questioning her motives, not to mention her sanity.

And as if he didn't feel like enough of a jerk, he kept playing over in his head what she said about the ranch. How he belonged there, and she wanted him to be happy. The truth is, she was way too good for him.

He sensed more than heard Ellie walk up. The woman gave off a vibe—*Look out, here comes trouble.*

She sat beside him in the grass and handed him one of the two beers she was holding.

"Thanks."

"Nice day," she said.

He took a deep swallow. "Hmm."

For a while she didn't say anything else. She just sat there beside him in companionable silence, sipping her beer, using whatever voodoo it was that compelled him to spill his guts when she knew he'd rather not talk about it. Like…mental Chinese water torture.

When the pressure got to be too much he finally said, "I suppose you want to know what happened."

She shrugged. "Only if you're ready to talk about it."

He wasn't. But only because he knew she would hit him with brutal honesty. She would walk through fire for him, but if she thought he was being a dufus, she wasn't shy about saying so.

And he was definitely a dufus.

"We had a fight."

"Did she break your heart?"

"No. But I'm pretty sure I broke hers."

She looked up at him, clearly confused. "Was it a preemptive strike? Because I was under the distinct impression that girl is crazy about you."

Twist the knife a little deeper.

"She's pregnant."

He braced for a lecture on the virtues of safe sex, or a demand that he do the right thing, but all she did was smile and say, "Grandma Ellie. That has a nice ring to it."

The woman never failed to surprise him. "You're not disappointed in me?"

"A baby is a blessing," she said, looking a little sad. An accident when she was a young girl prevented her from ever having kids of her own. But the truth was, she had been more of a mother to him than his own mother ever had.

"I asked her to marry me."

She nodded, like she had expected as much. "She turned you down."

He turned to look at her. "You don't seem surprised. I thought she was crazy about me."

"She's a smart girl. Why would she marry a man she barely

knows? And why would you ask her when she doesn't even know your real name?"

"I thought you would be happy that I tried to do the right thing."

"Marriage is not always the right thing. Look at your parents. Do you honestly think they were better off for it?"

The question stung a little, but she was right. He looked over at his mother's tombstone.

Loving wife and mother.

Far from it. As a wife she had been suspicious and neurotic. As a mother, vacant at best.

"You know, one of these days you're going to have to forgive her," Ellie said. "And yourself."

"If I had gone upstairs just ten minutes sooner…"

"You might have saved her. That time. But there would have been another time, Brandon." She paused then added, "There always was."

He closed his eyes, braced himself against the burn in his heart. He had always suspected there had been other attempts. He recalled vaguely from his childhood, times when she had been gone for a week or two. "Your mother isn't feeling well," his father used to say.

No one had ever come right out and admitted it. Until now. He could have asked. Maybe he should have. Or maybe he just didn't want to face the truth. Maybe it had been easier to blame his father for all of their problems, to channel all the disappointment and anger at a living, breathing target.

"She was a lousy mother, yet I'm still furious with her for abandoning me. She was self-centered, and narcissistic—"

"And sick, Brandon. Your mother was a very sick woman. You have to let it go."

"I'm trying."

She took a swallow of her beer. "Clint says you heard from that accountant you hired to look over the Hannah's Hope financial records."

He nodded. "He called yesterday afternoon."

"Did he tell you what you wanted to hear?"

"He told me what I expected to hear."

"So you're going through with it? Your grand announcement."

"That's the plan." He'd come this far, there was no backing out now. Besides, what he had to say *needed* to be heard.

She nodded thoughtfully, then glanced over at him and grinned.

"What?"

She reached up and patted the cleanly shaven cheek, rumpled his freshly cut hair like he was ten years old again. "It's good to have the old Brandon back."

"It's good to be back." Although somehow home didn't feel the same anymore. And he was pretty sure it wouldn't until Paige was at his side.

So maybe it was time he stopped sitting around feeling sorry for himself and did something about it.

Fifteen

So far the gala had gone exactly as planned, even better than Paige had hoped. Except that Brandon hadn't shown up yet. It was nearly time for him to accept his award and he was nowhere to be found. Paige had tried his cell phone at least a dozen times but he wasn't answering. She'd called the ranch and Ellie said he'd left hours ago. Since then she'd been nervously watching the door. She knew he was upset, but he had an obligation to Hannah's Hope. He simply had to show up. If not for her, then for the people who had volunteered their time to help him.

Ana approached Paige, looking anxious. "Have you heard from him?"

She shook her head. This was all her fault. If she had only waited to tell Brandon about the baby until after the gala—or if she hadn't started seeing him in the first place—this wouldn't be happening.

Emma—who after last night Paige now counted as a dear

friend—waddled over and introduced Paige to Chase Larson, her husband.

"Great party," Chase told Paige, shaking her hand, and said with a grin, "You've made quite an impression on my wife. Emma has decided that we need to have a party just so we can hire you to organize it."

"I would be honored. In fact, I have a few really cool theme ideas I could show you."

"I'll call you first thing Monday and we'll set up a time," Emma said, then asked, "Feeling a little better tonight?"

Physically, yes, because she'd been careful about what she ate, but emotionally she was a wreck. "I'm nervous about seeing him again."

Emma took her hand and gave it a squeeze. "It'll be okay, I promise."

She looked so earnest, Paige almost believed her, then Ward Miller's band started their set, which was loud enough to make talking nearly impossible. Ward wowed the crowd with a few of his biggest hits while Ana looked on proudly, then he wowed the crowd further with a substantial donation from the Cara Miller Foundation.

"Awesome party!" Gillian Preston gushed, approaching Paige near the buffet table as she was checking that the appetizers were being replenished. "Have you met my husband, Max?"

Paige shook his hand. "A pleasure to meet you."

"You've made Rafe a very happy man," Max said with a warm smile. "He has a lot riding on this and you're making him look very good. I assure you he won't forget it."

"And I'm going to write a piece for the *Seaside Gazette* that will have everyone champing at the bit to hire you for their next event," Gillian said.

"That would be really awesome," Paige said, basking in the glow of her accomplishment, even when inside she still felt tied in knots.

At least something in her life was going really well. And if Brandon couldn't find it in his heart to forgive her, her success would give her and the baby the financial security they needed. Rafe Cameron even took a minute away from schmoozing with potential donors to tell her how pleased he was with the party, and that he would definitely be using her services again in the future. The night was barely half over and already it had been more of a success than she could have ever hoped. But for the chance to be with Brandon, she would happily leave it all behind. She just hoped he would give her one more chance.

"Paige?"

The deep rumble of Brandon's voice coming from behind her plucked every one of Paige's frayed nerve endings. She'd been dying to see him, and now she was scared to death.

She turned slowly, both anticipating and dreading this, and when her eyes landed on the man standing behind her, her jaw dropped.

"Brandon?"

He had shaved, and cut his hair. And he looked so gorgeous in his tux that her heart actually stung. And though she hadn't meant to do it here, the words just sort of gushed out. "I am *so* sorry."

"No, I am," he said, then he reached for her, and she didn't care who saw them, or her professional image. She threw herself in his arms and hugged him tight.

She pressed her face to his chest, breathed him in. God, this was so good. So right. How could she have ever doubted him? She had to fight the tears of relief welling in her eyes. "I thought you weren't coming."

"I just needed some time." He cupped her cheek in his rough palm, lifted her face to his. "I missed you."

"I missed you, too. And I didn't mean anything I said. You just surprised me. Then I got scared."

"I know. I blindsided you, then I didn't give you a chance to explain."

"It was never about the money."

"I know." He lowered his head and brushed his lips over hers. It felt a little strange without the facial hair, yet deliciously familiar.

"Is there somewhere we could go to talk?" he asked.

"There's no time now. You're due on stage any minute."

"Brandon!" Ana said, scurrying up to them. "Thank God, you made it." She stopped short and looked him up and down. "Wow, nice threads. Paige must have gotten one hell of a deal."

Puzzled, Paige stepped back and took in his clothing. This was definitely not the tux they had ordered. In fact, she would bet it wasn't even a rental. The silk was exquisite, and she was guessing by the precise fit it had to be custom-made.

"Where did you get this?" she asked.

"Long story. That's why we need to talk." He asked Ana, "Could you give us two minutes?"

"Two minutes," she said, hurrying off in the direction of the stage.

"Brandon, what's going on?" Paige asked.

He took a deep breath and blew it out. "Okay, here's the thing—"

"Brandon? Is that you?"

Paige turned to see Emma standing behind her, eyes wide with surprise.

"Emma," Brandon said.

They shared an awkward embrace and Emma said, "What are you doing here?"

"Long story."

Now Paige was totally confused. "You two know each other?"

"Of course we know each other," Emma said.

"But…we talked about him last night and you never said anything about knowing him."

Now Emma looked confused. "We did?"

"Yes, this is Brandon Dilson."

"Paige, this is Brandon *Worth,* my brother."

Her *brother?* Paige looked up at Brandon for an explanation.

"Like I said, it's a long story."

Emma gasped suddenly. "Oh, my God! My *brother* is the father of your baby?"

Paige blinked. Brandon Dilson was really Brandon Worth? Not an uneducated ranch hand, but heir to the Worth millions? All this time he'd been lying to her?

"I—I don't understand," Paige said.

"I know, and I can explain everything."

"Brandon," Ana said, rejoining them. "We need you on stage. Now."

"On stage?" Emma asked. "Did you make a contribution to the foundation?"

Brandon looked from Paige to Ana, then back to his sister. "It's really—"

Emma held up a hand to cut him off. "A long story."

Brandon turned to Paige, gripping her upper arms firmly. "This isn't the way I wanted you to hear this, but do me a favor. No matter what, don't leave until I've said everything I have to say up there."

"Of course." She wanted to know what the hell was going on.

He gave her a quick, firm kiss, then followed Ana. Paige and Emma both pushed their way closer to the stage. Rafe was at the mic, and when he saw Brandon approaching he made his announcement.

"Ladies and gentlemen, I am pleased and honored to present the recipient of the Hannah's Hope Outstanding Achievement Award, Mr. Brandon Dilson."

The crowd broke into applause as Brandon crossed the stage to the mic, with the confidence of a man who was used to being the center of attention. He and Rafe shook hands, but when he held out the plaque Brandon was supposed to accept, Brandon shook his head. Rafe frowned, looking confused, and around her, Paige heard baffled whispers.

Brandon stepped up to the mic. "Thank you Mr. Cameron, but I'm afraid I can't accept this award."

Quiet gasps filled the room.

"As some of you may have figured out by now, my last name is not Dilson, it's Worth. I was, until a few months ago, heir to Worth Industries. I've spent the past four months posing as Brandon Dilson, an uneducated ranch hand, for the sole purpose of infiltrating Hannah's Hope and discrediting the foundation and its founder, Rafe Cameron."

The crowd erupted in chatter and Rafe advanced in his direction, but, nonplussed, Brandon held up a hand to halt him.

"Please," he said over the din, "allow me to explain."

A hush fell over the audience.

"When I learned that my father's company was bought by Cameron Enterprises, in what some have termed a hostile takeover, needless to say I was concerned. Anyone familiar with our families knows there's history there. Then rumors began to circulate that Mr. Cameron's intention was to break the company into pieces and sell it to the highest bidder, which everyone here knows would devastate the economy of Vista del Mar. That factory has been this city's lifeline for generations. And because I chose not to take my rightful place by my father's side, I held myself personally responsible. I vowed to discredit Rafe Cameron, to give the people of the city a chance, and Hannah's Hope seemed the way to do it."

Brandon's gaze fixed on the audience to the right of where Paige stood, and she glanced over to see Ronald Worth, Brandon's father, standing beside Emma. The two men locked gazes, and there was a hurt in their eyes that was almost palpable.

Paige had heard things mentioned about Ronald Worth's

estranged son. Never in a million years would she have guessed that it was Brandon.

"I did it for the people of Vista del Mar, and for the factory employees, but I've also come to realize that even more than that, I did it for myself. To reconcile the guilt I've felt for abandoning my family. And I *did* abandon them."

Beside Paige, Emma sniffed and dabbed at her eyes, and her father slipped an arm around her shoulders. If there was one thing Paige knew about Brandon, it was that he was a proud man. Pouring out his heart in front of everyone couldn't have been easy for him, and his family seemed to appreciate that.

"I have spent the last four months investigating every aspect of Hannah's Hope. I've dug through city and county records, exhausted every resource available, and I am here to report that Hannah's Hope is one hundred percent legitimate. The service they have provided to the people of this community is beyond reproach. In the time I've been working with the organization, I've seen men and women whose lives have been transformed by the mentors who selflessly volunteer their time. I for one will be pulling out my checkbook for a substantial donation, and I encourage you all to do the same." Brandon turned to face Rafe. "I hope that Rafe and Ana and the mentor who sacrificed his own time to tutor me, will accept my most heartfelt apology. I also want to say I'm sorry to my family for…well, for more things than I have time to list." His eyes settled on Paige. "And Paige Adams, who just so happens to be the woman who single-handedly planned this outstanding party, I just want to say that I love you. And though I know I screwed up, and I have no right to ask this, I hope you'll give me one more chance."

Tears stung the corners of Paige's eyes. He'd told her he loved her, and managed a pretty awesome plug for her company in the same breath.

Brandon turned to Rafe to shake his hand, and for several seconds Rafe only glared at him. The crowd waited in tense silence, and Rafe looked so bitter that for a horrifying moment Paige thought they might come to blows. Finally, Rafe took his hand for a brief, brusque shake, and the audience erupted in applause. Brandon said a few brief words to a shell-shocked Ana, then exited the stage and walked over to where Paige still stood with his sister and father.

"Brandon," Ronald said, shaking his hand, then he pulled him into a slightly awkward, but heartfelt embrace. "It's good to see you, son."

"You, too," Brandon said, and Paige saw that both men's eyes had misted over.

They parted and Brandon said, "You look good."

The older man smiled. "I feel good. I wasn't crazy about the idea of retiring, but I think it was time. This is the healthiest I've felt in years."

"I'm glad to hear it. You've earned the right to relax."

"Things are going well at Copper Run?"

"Great. You should visit some time."

"I'll do that." He turned to Paige and said with a grin, "And this must be Paige Adams, the woman responsible for this outstanding party."

Paige could see where Brandon inherited his charm. She shook his hand and said, "It's nice to meet you."

"My daughter tells me that you two are expecting a child."

Paige nodded. "January twenty-second."

Brandon looked down at her and laughed. "You're kidding."

"That's Brandon's birthday," Emma said.

"And mine," Paige told her.

Brandon shook his head. "What are the odds?"

"Astronomical." She smiled up at him. "I guess it's fate."

"I hope this means you'll visit more," Emma said. "I want to see my niece or nephew."

"And I want to see mine," Brandon said, patting her belly.

"So, are there any wedding plans in the future?" Ronald asked.

Brandon took Paige's hand. "Actually, that's something that Paige and I need to talk about."

"Then we should leave you two alone," Ronald said.

"We'll talk," Brandon told him.

Ronald nodded. "I think it's past time, don't you?"

Emma pulled Paige into an embrace and whispered, "Welcome to the family."

After they walked away Brandon said, "Let's go somewhere a bit more private."

"That was a good thing you did up there," she told him as he led her toward the French doors.

"It was the truth," he said. "It wasn't easy getting up there and admitting I was wrong, but I had to do it."

"You probably won't like this, but the rumour is that Rafe stills plans to break the company apart and sell off the pieces. I heard someone say that there's going to be a front-page article about it in the *Seaside Gazette* tomorrow."

He looked more resigned than angry. "Unfortunately, at this point there isn't anything anyone can do. And right now, our relationship is my number one priority."

She felt exactly the same way. Her career, and those goals she'd worked on so hard for so many years to achieve seemed inconsequential now.

He opened the door for her and they stepped out onto the slate patio, lit only by the full moon and a sky full of stars, and her heart started to beat like mad. He said he loved her, and he wanted to talk about marriage. And this time she wouldn't screw it up and say the wrong thing.

As soon as the door shut behind them he pulled her into his arms and just held her. "I missed you so much."

She closed her eyes and hugged him hard. "Me, too."

"I'm so sorry that I lied to you."

She looked up at him. "You were doing what you thought you had to."

"That doesn't make it right."

"But it's forgivable. And I forgive you."

"And the other day, at the motel, I wasn't fair."

She shrugged. "It doesn't matter. It's done."

"I told you we should get married because it was what was best for the baby. What I should have said, what I was afraid to admit, is that I want to marry you because I *love* you."

She reached up and touched his smooth cheek. "I love you, too. I didn't mean for it to happen. It just did."

"My head is telling me that you were right to say no. That it's too soon to be making that sort of commitment."

Her heart sank.

"It's telling me that we should give it some time, get to know one another."

A very logical course of action, so why did she feel so lousy?

Brandon reached up and touched her cheek. "But my heart, that's telling me that you're the woman I'm supposed to spend the rest of my life with, and a couple of months won't change that. So, Paige Adams..." He sank down on one knee. "Would you—"

"Yes!" She threw her arms around his neck and hugged him. "Yes, yes, yes."

Brandon laughed. "So I guess that's a yes."

"Definitely."

"Then you'll probably be wanting this," he said, and pulled a diamond solitaire ring from his jacket pocket. A huge, *gorgeous* ring.

She gasped. "It's beautiful."

"Before I put this on your finger, there's a disclaimer. This was my mother's ring, and anyone will tell you that she was a little kooky. So I'm giving you the option. You can wear this, or we can go out first thing tomorrow and buy you something new."

She knew he wouldn't have asked her to wear it if it didn't mean a great deal to him. Besides, what ring she wore didn't matter, she was his, and he was hers. For better or worse, richer or poorer.

She smiled and held out her hand, and he slipped the ring on....

* * * * *

What made Rafe Cameron so ruthless?
Could lost hopes and dreams from his high school
graduation night play a part?

Turn the page for an exclusive short story
by USA TODAY bestselling author Catherine Mann.
Then look for the story of Rafe and Sarah's reunion in
ACQUIRED: THE CEO'S SMALL-TOWN BRIDE
by Catherine Mann,
the finale of THE TAKEOVER miniseries,
wherever Harlequin books are sold.

14 years ago

"Parents, family, friends, I present to you this year's graduating class of Vista del Mar High School."

Along with all her classmates, Sarah Richards pitched her gold-tasseled hat up into the air. Then she hitched up her gown and started pushing through the crowd and darting around the empty folding chairs. Who cared about getting the silly old cap back? She just wanted to hug Rafe.

Finally, they'd made it. They were both eighteen. They had high school diplomas. They could really be together now.

Stretching up onto her toes, she looked over the heads of graduates and families. Across the gymnasium, she saw his blond hair in the distance. The halogen bulbs overhead glinted off the natural highlights he'd gotten from working so hard at his construction job after school. Love bubbled up inside her. She was so proud to call him her boyfriend.

Since everyone was seated alphabetically, there were lots

of folks between where she sat as a Richards and he sat as a Cameron. But she didn't even question if the top of a head she saw was really him. She knew Rafe, *her* Rafe.

Her feet raced as fast as her heart. She angled sideways.

"Excuse me, please." She smiled as she passed Quentin Dobbs's parents trying to push through to their son.

An arm slid around her shoulders and she stopped short. Her father, mother and Grandma Kat were all holding programs and grinning from ear to ear. God, she was going to miss them when she left. If she could just talk Rafe into picking someplace a little closer than Los Angeles so it wouldn't cost so much gas money to get home.

Home. Her happy mood dimmed.

She had to get used to thinking of somewhere else as home. Rafe was going to be her new safe harbor, forever. Still, she looked around at her familiar school, her family, her friends. The town she'd called home all her life.

She swallowed down a wad of tears fast. She didn't want to answer a bunch of uncomfortable questions before she and Rafe had firmed up their plans. They'd been fighting a lot this past month about whether they would spend the summer here or leave right away. They'd fought hardest about where to go when the time came. She loved him so much, but she was getting scared if she didn't act fast, she would lose him.

Her throat threatened to close up. She forced a smile for her family.

"Hi, Daddy." She kissed her father on his leathery cheek. "I'm so glad you could get the time off from the factory to be here."

"Wouldn't have missed this for anything. We're so proud of you, baby." Her dad hugged her, his wiry red hair standing up in sprigs in the back. Then he passed her over to her mom and grandmother.

Her parents worked the evening shift at Worth Industries, Vista del Mar's only real factory. They pulled lots of overtime, too. Having Grandma Kat on call at night for free sitting had offered them options since Sarah was a toddler. Was it any wonder she was especially close to her grandma after all the time they'd spent together?

As she hugged her grandmother extra tight, Sarah caught a clearer view of Rafe.

He was shrugging out of his graduation gown and accepting his congrats from Bob and Penny and Penny's son, Chase. Rafe said he'd only marched because it was important to his dad. He would have just as soon blown off the whole thing, but since Bob hadn't gotten his GED until recently, it was a big deal that his son finished on time, at eighteen.

"Sarah?" Her grandmother's voice drew her eyes away from Rafe.

"Yes, Grandma Kat? Sorry, I was, uh…"

"I can see exactly what you were doing," Kathleen said with a knowing smile. She'd softened up a little when it came to Rafe. About time. "Why don't you go over and speak to him?"

She started to accept the offer so she could race right over. But then she looked at her parents, all dressed up and taking an evening off work to be here.

Her parents were quieter than Grandma Kat and she were. And even though she felt closer to her grandmother, she still loved her folks.

Soon, she would have all the time in the world with Rafe and none with her family. "It's okay, Grandma. He and I have plans later tonight, with the graduation party and all."

Okay, that part was a lie. Rafe didn't want any part of a celebration like that. She would have liked to go, just to say unofficial goodbyes to everyone. But in the end, Rafe was what mattered.

Tonight mattered.

Because tonight, once they were away from the ceremony

and alone together, she was going to tell Rafe she would leave town with him as soon as he was ready.

Parked in Rafe's El Camino on Busted Bluff, Sarah sighed as the last ripples of release shimmered through her. Her arm slid to the floor, Rafe still on top of her, his hand between her legs.

They'd gotten really good at finishing each other without actually doing everything. As much as she wanted to take that final step, she was still kind of nervous.

At first, that had been an amazing relief, orgasms anytime she wanted them with the hottest guy in the world. But already a new frenzy was building with the increasing need to have him inside her.

She slid her hands inside his open jeans and cupped his butt. His amazing butt. "I want us to leave town this week. Together. We can go to L.A., or anywhere else that you want. I'll be happy as long as I'm with you."

Maybe if she said that enough times she wouldn't be scared to death.

Rafe shifted off her, his eyes wide with shock as he sat up. He didn't get surprised very often. She enjoyed knowing that for once she wasn't the only person knocked off balance by all the changes in their lives.

"You really mean that?" he asked warily, zipping his pants again, adjusting the polo shirt he'd worn under the cap and gown at graduation.

"Why? Did you not really want me to go with you?" She hadn't even considered that possibility, a notion that took her fears to a whole new level.

"I asked, didn't I?" He scowled.

Her feelings more than a little hurt, she tugged her dress back over her knees and kicked her pink panties under the seat. "You don't sound all that enthusiastic."

He studied her for a minute by the glow of the dashboard

lights, crossing his arms over his chest before speaking. "I think you have a glorified idea of what it's going to be like. You already complain about how we don't spend much time together now. It's going to be worse when we're actually paying rent on a place."

"Complain?" Anger began to overshadow her hurt feelings. "You think I *complain?*"

"Are you spoiling for a fight?" he asked too damn calmly.

Maybe. Probably. "I'm just nervous about the decisions we're making. My parents work all the time. I understand we need the money, but for as long as I can remember they have pulled the evening shift, leaving Grandma Kat to watch over me, tuck me in when I was in elementary school, fix my hair for the prom. When we go away together, I don't want to live that way anymore, not with you."

She didn't want their kids to live that way. But talking about kids and how expensive they were would really freak him out.

"Sarah, I'm working this hard so that won't happen."

"That's what my folks said." She gripped his shirt, desperate to make him understand. "Tomorrow was always going to be better. But here I am graduating from high school and things still haven't changed at my house."

"I guess you'll just have to trust me then, won't you?" His hands covered hers. "Because there's only one other choice. Not being together at all."

Panic squeezed her ribs at talk of not being together. "You really think you can't get ahead if we go to one of the smaller towns?"

He sighed heavily. "I thought you said you were willing to go to L.A."

"I am," she rushed to reassure him.

"It's the right choice, you know." He brought her hands to his lips. "Did your parents get ahead staying here in Vista del Mar their whole lives?"

He had a point, and his point scared her because she realized there really might not be a compromise. Tears burned her eyes.

She eased her hands from his and scrubbed her wrist along her cheeks, smearing a little mascara on the back of her hand. "I've never lived anywhere else before. I'll feel better once we've settled where we're going to be."

"Los Angeles—"

"Los Angeles. Right." She nodded, her jaw trembling just a little. "For real. The two of us."

He swept her into his arms with a whoop of happiness, then kissed her. It was so rare to see Rafe happy. The move would be all right. It had to be.

Rafe angled her back on the seat, tucking her under him. His kisses grew more intense, more persuasive as he nipped along her jaw, her collarbone. Further. Until the shoulders of her dress were down and he had his mouth all over her. She was almost climbing out of her skin with the need to be with him. Fully. The past month, giving each other release in every manner possible other than going all the way was starting to get frustrating.

She didn't know how much longer she could hold out. His hand slid up her dress, along her thigh. As much as she wanted to be with him, a part of her was still so hurt that he couldn't see his way clear to find a compromise. Why did she have to be the one to give in on everything? If he could just give her some sign to show her he was as committed to making a life together as she was…

He bunched the hem of her dress in his hands, higher and higher, air brushing between her thighs since her panties were still somewhere under the seat. Rafe kissed along her neck just the way she liked most, whispering in her ear how hot she made him, how much he wanted her.

So many words and not one of them having anything to do with love.

"I love you, Rafe." Her fingernails dug into his shoulders.

"I love you, too, Kitten," he said, but it sounded kinda automatic, and he seemed a lot more focused on pushing down the top of her dress. "And God, I want you so damn much it hurts."

"I want you, too. But I want us to be married first." The words fell out in a rush before she even really thought about them.

Rafe went very still on top of her.

The air went quiet all around them until she couldn't tell whose heart was thumping louder, hers or his. She looked up into his eyes, hating that she felt hesitant, but no way was she going to pull back the words now that they were out there. She was making big changes in her life for him. Was it so wrong of her to want a sign of commitment from him in return? "Aren't you going to say anything?"

Still, he didn't move, just stayed stretched out over her, his face all emotionless. "You want us to get married before we have sex, before we can go to L.A.?"

Yep. Pretty much.

"Call me an old-fashioned dinosaur if you want, but I can't go all that way and just move in with you." What if he dumped her and she was stuck in that big city with nothing, not even him? "It wouldn't feel right to me."

His chest heaved with a huge sigh, then he nodded as he rolled off her and back into the driver's seat. "Okay then. Let's elope. Tonight."

Rafe pulled up outside the Any Day Wedding Chapel outside of San Diego, his rusty El Camino just about on empty. But they'd made it. Sarah was nearly levitating off her seat with happiness. He tugged at his collar.

Lights from the little white chapel blink, blink, blinked, except the "W" was burned out. The lot was filled with about a dozen other cars parked haphazardly by people apparently as impetuous as Sarah and he were. It was graduation night at a lot of high schools in the area and apparently they weren't the only ones who'd come up with this reckless idea.

Two couples charged up the stairs lined with plastic flowers, at least one of them was drunk. This wasn't what he'd planned for when he thought of marrying Sarah. And yeah, he'd thought about it, especially over the past month. Except she wasn't leaving him much choice on how this played out, and bottom line, he didn't want to lose her.

So, he was really going to do this. He was going to marry Sarah tonight.

He pulled his hand out of his pocket and held up a thin gold band—his mother's ring. His dad had given it to him a while back, said it was his to do with as he wished. That even if he needed to pawn it someday, Hannah would be cool with that. She'd only wanted the best for her son.

Luckily, when he'd stopped by the house to get the ring, his dad had still been out with Penny and Chase. Rafe placed the band in Sarah's palm.

"It was my mom's," he said, his throat tight.

Her hands shook and her eyes filled with tears. "It's lovely and so very special. Rafe, I don't even know what to say."

"It doesn't have a stone or anything, but I'll get you the biggest diamond set to replace it one day."

"You will not." She folded her hand over his. "This ring will stay on my finger forever."

Forever. He would have been happier if forever started when he had more than five hundred bucks saved up, not nearly enough for a decent safe place to live and reliable wheels for both of them. His mind started churning with the practical things Sarah seemed to just brush aside with that amazing smile of hers. A smile that made him do very impractical things.

"You can keep the ring, but I'm still going to add diamonds to it, huge ones that will make even Ronald Worth sit up and take notice."

She clapped a hand over his mouth. "Can we please not bring up Mr. Worth? Not tonight. Honestly, as long as I have you, that's all I need."

"You're so naive sometimes." The words fell out of his mouth before he could think.

"Don't be a jerk." She thumped him on the shoulder. "I refuse to let you wreck this night for me. We're going to get married, remember? We're really going to be husband and wife by morning."

His libido gave a great big throbbing shout of encouragement. He slid his hand behind her neck and brought her to him. Kissing her, taking in the familiar taste and feel of her, he could forget all the rest. Maybe if they had sex, lots and lots of sex, he could shut up the doubt demons. Sounded like a plan to him.

Sighing that kittenish sound that always drove him crazy, Sarah eased back, her hands flat on his chest.

She stared up into his eyes, her green eyes reflecting the stars overhead. "Tell me you love me. I know you think words are silly, but I need to hear them."

"I love you, Sarah," he said automatically, already angling to kiss her again, to get as close to her as he could in the confines of his car.

Her eyebrows pinched together and he realized he must have screwed up somehow. Damn, but women were tough to figure out.

She nibbled her bottom lip. "You don't want to do this, do you?"

"Of course I want to be with you." He dodged her real question. "I don't want to leave you in Vista del Mar, and God, I don't want to wait another second to be with you."

"That's not the same as wanting to marry me." She studied him with a wisdom, a seriousness he hadn't seen before.

"I do want to marry you."

"Just not now," she pressed.

All the tension of the past five months built inside him. He'd been trying to plan out his life but dating Sarah had knocked everything off-kilter. "I would be lying if I said this was an ideal set up. Why would I *want* to give you a tacky quickie ceremony?" His frustration, his anger at the whole damn unfair world rose with each word. "Why would I want to take my bride to a crappy one-room apartment in the worst section of town? But there aren't a lot of options here until I start making serious money."

"I'm in your way." The starlight faded from her eyes.

"Damn it, Sarah." He clasped her shoulders. "Don't put it like that."

"You don't want to get married."

He stayed silent this time.

She looked at the ring in her hand, then pressed it into his palm and folded his fingers over it. "I'll make this easier for you. We're not getting married. Go to Los Angeles and follow your dreams. Mine are in Vista del Mar."

She leaned across the seat and pressed her lips to his, holding, not moving, her eyes squeezed shut and a single tear escaping. "I'm going to get out of the car now and I do not want you to follow me. I'm going to call my grandmother for a ride. And I mean it. I don't want to see you again. I can't. Goodbye, Rafe."

She slipped out of the car and into the wedding chapel. Relief jockeyed with regret in his gut. He didn't follow her inside, but he would wait around just out of sight to make sure her grandmother arrived safely. After that, he was leaving for Los Angeles. He had five hundred bucks saved up.

This wasn't goodbye, damn it. He would be back for her, once he made enough money to give her a safer, more secure life. She wouldn't have to wait long. Just three years, four at the most until he could work while going to night school. He wouldn't last longer than that without her anyway.

And God forbid some other guy try to step into his place.

Because he would be back. And when he returned, he would claim Sarah as his wife.

* * * * *

Harlequin Desire

COMING NEXT MONTH

Available June 14, 2011

#2089 THE PROPOSAL
Brenda Jackson
The Westmorelands

#2090 ACQUIRED: THE CEO'S SMALL-TOWN BRIDE
Catherine Mann
The Takeover

#2091 HER LITTLE SECRET, HIS HIDDEN HEIR
Heidi Betts
Billionaires and Babies

#2092 THE BILLIONAIRE'S BEDSIDE MANNER
Robyn Grady

#2093 AT HIS MAJESTY'S CONVENIENCE
Jennifer Lewis
Royal Rebels

#2094 MEDDLING WITH A MILLIONAIRE
Cat Schield

HDCNM0511

REQUEST YOUR FREE BOOKS!

2 FREE NOVELS PLUS 2 FREE GIFTS!

Harlequin® Desire

ALWAYS POWERFUL, PASSIONATE AND PROVOCATIVE

YES! Please send me 2 FREE Harlequin Desire® novels and my 2 FREE gifts (gifts are worth about $10). After receiving them, if I don't wish to receive any more books, I can return the shipping statement marked "cancel." If I don't cancel, I will receive 6 brand-new novels every month and be billed just $4.05 per book in the U.S. or $4.74 per book in Canada. That's a saving of at least 15% off the cover price! It's quite a bargain! Shipping and handling is just 50¢ per book in the U.S. and 75¢ per book in Canada.* I understand that accepting the 2 free books and gifts places me under no obligation to buy anything. I can always return a shipment and cancel at any time. Even if I never buy another book, the two free books and gifts are mine to keep forever.

225/326 SDN FC65

Name _____ (PLEASE PRINT) _____

Address _____ Apt. #

City _____ State/Prov. _____ Zip/Postal Code

Signature (if under 18, a parent or guardian must sign)

Mail to the **Reader Service:**
IN U.S.A.: P.O. Box 1867, Buffalo, NY 14240-1867
IN CANADA: P.O. Box 609, Fort Erie, Ontario L2A 5X3

Not valid for current subscribers to Harlequin Desire books.

Want to try two free books from another line?
Call 1-800-873-8635 or visit www.ReaderService.com.

* Terms and prices subject to change without notice. Prices do not include applicable taxes. Sales tax applicable in N.Y. Canadian residents will be charged applicable taxes. Offer not valid in Quebec. This offer is limited to one order per household. All orders subject to credit approval. Credit or debit balances in a customer's account(s) may be offset by any other outstanding balance owed by or to the customer. Please allow 4 to 6 weeks for delivery. Offer available while quantities last.

Your Privacy—The Reader Service is committed to protecting your privacy. Our Privacy Policy is available online at www.ReaderService.com or upon request from the Reader Service.

We make a portion of our mailing list available to reputable third parties that offer products we believe may interest you. If you prefer that we not exchange your name with third parties, or if you wish to clarify or modify your communication preferences, please visit us at www.ReaderService.com/consumerchoice or write to us at Reader Service Preference Service, P.O. Box 9062, Buffalo, NY 14269. Include your complete name and address.

HDES11

Harlequin® Blaze™ brings you
New York Times *and* **USA TODAY** *bestselling author*
Vicki Lewis Thompson with three new steamy titles
from the bestselling miniseries SONS OF CHANCE

Chance isn't just the last name of these rugged
Wyoming cowboys—it's their motto, too!

Read on for a sneak peek at the first title,
SHOULD'VE BEEN A COWBOY

Available June 2011 only from Harlequin® Blaze™.

"THANKS FOR NOT TURNING ON THE LIGHTS," Tyler said. "I'm a mess."

"Not in my book." Even in low light, Alex had a good view of her yellow shirt plastered to her body. It was all he could do not to reach for her, mud and all. But the next move needed to be hers, not his.

She slicked her wet hair back and squeezed some water out of the ends as she glanced upward. "I like the sound of the rain on a tin roof."

"Me, too."

She met his gaze briefly and looked away. "Where's the sink?"

"At the far end, beyond the last stall."

Tyler's running shoes squished as she walked down the aisle between the rows of stalls. She glanced sideways at Alex. "So how much of a cowboy are you these days? Do you ride the range and stuff?"

"I ride." He liked being able to say that. "Why?"

"Just wondered. Last summer, you were still a city boy. You even told me you weren't the cowboy type, but you're…different now."

He wasn't sure if that was a good thing or a bad thing. Maybe she preferred city boys to cowboys. "How am I different?"

"Well, you dress differently, and your hair's a little longer. Your face seems a little more chiseled, but maybe that's because of your hair. Also, there's something else, something harder to define, an attitude…"

"Are you saying I have an attitude?"

"Not in a bad way. It's more like a quiet confidence."

He was flattered, but still he had to laugh. "I just admitted a while ago that I have all kinds of doubts about this event tomorrow. That doesn't seem like quiet confidence to me."

"This isn't about your job, it's about…your…" She took a deep breath. "It's about your sex appeal, okay? I have no business talking about it, because it will only make me want to do things I shouldn't do." She started toward the end of the barn. "Now, where's that sink? We need to get cleaned up and go back to the house. Dinner is probably ready, and I—"

He spun her around and pulled her into his arms, mud and all. "Let's do those things." Then he kissed her, knowing that she would kiss him back, knowing that this time he would take that kiss where he wanted it to go. And she would let him.

Follow Tyler and Alex's wild adventures in
SHOULD'VE BEEN A COWBOY
Available June 2011 only from Harlequin® Blaze™
wherever books are sold.